MASTER LISTS FOR WRITERS

THESAURUSES, PLOTS, CHARACTER TRAITS, NAMES, AND MORE

BRYN DONOVAN

D1160729

Master Lists for Writers
Copyright 2015 by Munds Park Publishing

All rights reserved
bryndonovan.com

First edition, October 2015
ISBN: 978-0-9967152-1-8

ACKNOWLEDGEMENTS

As I wrote this book, I was blessed with the enthusiastic moral support of my family, my "real life" friends, including the Scoobies, and my online communities—the Lentils, the Binders, and the NaNoWriMo group. I appreciate you all so much.

I also want to thank the readers and followers of my blog, bryndonovan.com. I would like to give special appreciation to Pulitzer Prize-winning poet Robert Hass for his permission to quote his poem in this book.

Most of all, I owe so much to Gill Donovan, a wonderful writer, a smart editor, the kindest human being I have ever met, and my soul mate. I love you, darling.

TABLE OF CONTENTS

INTRODUCTION

Welcome to *Master Lists for Writers*!

A couple of years ago, I started making lists to help me with writing projects. They included titles I might use someday, words for love scenes, medieval figures of speech, and ways to describe emotions. Essentially, they were specialized thesauruses.

When I started my blog, I shared some of my writing lists, and lots of people told me how useful they were. That inspired me to create this book.

To tell the truth, even as a little kid, I always loved making lists. They are exercises in thinking about all the possibilities, and as an optimist, that appeals to me. Additionally, I've always had the strong urge to help other people's creative projects succeed.

Some people have referred to my lists as "cheat sheets." I'm happy that they make writing faster and easier, because that was my intention. However, I don't think you're cheating by using this book! We all get inspiration and solutions from many sources—TV, movies, books, websites, conversations, and observations of real life. This book is just one additional resource.

If you find the perfect solution in here when you're stuck, please feel free to apply it directly. That's what the book is for. Chances are, you'll have to either change it a bit or expand upon it to fit your writing. Even if you don't, it's a drop of water in the big sea of your story. It will blend in, and you'll make it your own.

On the other hand, reading a list may make you think of a new solution that isn't even on the page. That's how lists work. For instance, when someone posts a top 10 list online, others usually chime in to ask, "But what about this one?" "How could you leave that one off?"

None of the lists in this book is comprehensive. In most cases, it would be impossible to make a complete list. You'll probably think of additions, which is part of the value of the book.

I want to make a note about pronouns. At first, I tried to use "they" as a singular, non-gendered pronoun everywhere. Because of the succinct format of lists, the use of "they" sometimes made things confusing, particularly in the section on plot ideas. I've chosen to use "he" and "she," mostly at random. Please remember that in every list, you can substitute any pronouns you like.

I hope this book is an inspiring, time-saving reference for you. Happy writing!

1. DESCRIPTIONS

It's very important for most readers to be able to picture characters and items in a scene clearly in their heads. Writers also need good descriptions of facial expressions, body language, and gestures to convey emotions and to set up lines of dialogue without always having to write "said" or any of its synonyms. Sometimes, we need fresh ways to describe emotions directly.

It's easy for us to rely on the same handful of descriptions. We can also lose our writing momentum when we take a long time trying to think of the right word or phrase. This section can make that process quicker and easier.

DESCRIPTIONS OF FACIAL EXPRESSIONS

I've categorized these expressions under "positive and neutral" (neutral meaning things like surprise and curiosity) and "negative." I haven't organized them according to particular emotion, because so many of them work for more than one. A person might narrow his eyes out of vindictiveness or skepticism, for instance, and his face might turn red out of anger or embarrassment.

Some of these require a little more explanation on your part. You'll have to say what she's glaring at, or if his face is contorting in rage, or grief, or what. And not all of these will work for every character—it depends on what the character looks like and how she generally reacts to things.

Some of these aren't *exactly* facial expressions, but still useful for dialogue tags. In many cases I've given several ways to describe the same thing. While I have included some longer phrases, they are not proprietary and it's fine to use them.

POSITIVE OR NEUTRAL EMOTIONS

These include, but aren't limited to, happiness, love, desire, amusement, and surprise.

she raised a brow	he lifted an eyebrow
his right eyebrow shot up	his eyebrows waggled
his eyes widened	her eyes bugged
his eyes lit up	her eyes darted
he squinted	she blinked
her eyes twinkled	his eyes gleamed

her eyes sparkled

her eyes glinted

her eyes blazed with...

her eyes flickered with...

lust glittered in her eyes

she winked

she batted her lashes

he sized her up

he eyed her

she slipped him a
curious glance

she slid him a guarded look

he gazed

he stared

he studied

he observed

she gawked

he gave her a puppy-dog look

her pupils were huge

he licked his lips

she smiled

his eyes flashed

his eyes burned with...

her eyes sparked with...

affection glowed in his eyes

the corners of his eyes crinkled

his lashes fluttered

she gave him a once-over

she took in the sight of...

she gave him a come-
hither look

he looked askance at her

she peered

she glanced

she scrutinized

she gaped

she surveyed

he leered

his pupils (were) dilated

his pupils flared

her lips parted

he smirked

she grinned

he simpered

she beamed

a smile danced on his lips

her mouth curved into a smile

the corners of his
mouth turned up

the corner of her
mouth quirked up

a smile tugged at his lips

a corner of her mouth lifted

his mouth twitched

he gave a half-smile

she gave a lopsided grin

he pursed his lips

she stuck out her tongue

her mouth fell open

his jaw dropped

her jaw went slack

her whole face lit up

she brightened

awe transformed his face

relief suffused his features

recognition dawned
on her face

his expression softened

NEGATIVE EMOTIONS

These include, but aren't limited to, sadness, anger, disgust, fear, anxiety, exhaustion, and embarrassment. Embarrassment can sometimes be positive, such as when a person gets a compliment that makes her blush, but I think it's more often negative.

his brows knitted

her forehead creased

his forehead furrowed

her forehead puckered

a line etched between
her brows

his brows drew together

her brows snapped together

his eyebrows rose

sweat beaded her forehead

perspiration shone on his brow

her face glistened with sweat

her eyes went round

terror flashed in his eyes

her eyelids drooped

his eyelids sagged

his eyes narrowed

she rolled her eyes

he looked heavenward

she glanced up at the ceiling

he avoided her gaze

his eyes had a haunted look

tears filled her eyes

his eyes welled up

her eyes swam with tears

his eyes flooded with tears

her eyes were wet

his eyes glistened

tears shimmered in her eyes

tears shone in his eyes

her eyes were glossy

he fought back tears

tears ran down her cheeks

his eyes closed

she squeezed her eyes shut

he shut his eyes

her eyes bored into him

she pinned him with her eyes

he stared

she gave him a frosty look

he cast her a veiled glance

her eyes shot sparks

he glared

her nose crinkled

his nose wrinkled

she sneered

his nostrils flared

she stuck her nose in the air

he sniffed

she sniffled

her upper lip curled

she forced a smile

her smile faded

she pouted

her mouth set in a hard line

she bit her lip

he chewed on his bottom lip

her jaw clenched

a muscle in her jaw twitched

he ground his jaw

her lips drew back in a snarl

her lower lip trembled

she paled

she went white

his face reddened

his face flushed

he turned red

he turned crimson

heat stained her cheeks

she scrunched up her face

his mouth twisted

he plastered on a smile

he faked a smile

his smile slipped

his mouth snapped shut

he pressed his lips together

she nibbled on her bottom lip

his jaw set

his jaw tightened

he gritted his teeth

he snarled

she gnashed her teeth

his lower lip quivered

he blanched

the color drained from his face

her cheeks turned pink

she blushed

she turned scarlet

a flush crept up her face

he screwed up his face

he had a hangdog expression

he grimaced

she gave him a dirty look

she scowled

his face went blank

his face twisted

his expression dulled

his expression sobered

a vein popped out in his neck

sadness clouded his features

she winced

he frowned

he glowered

her face contorted

her expression closed up

her expression hardened

she went poker-faced

fear crossed her face

terror overtook his face

DESCRIPTIONS OF GESTURES
AND BODY LANGUAGE

Many of these can mean different emotions in different contexts. Your heroine might lift her chin in confidence or in angry defiance. Your villain might rub his hands together because he's planning evil things or because it's cold in his lair. For that reason, I haven't attempted to separate these into positive and negative emotions.

Some of the things in my list are not exactly body language or gestures, but are useful for setting up dialogue. As with the list of facial expressions, I've included some different ways to say the same thing.

Each of your characters may have one or two gestures that are typical of him or her. While you wouldn't want to overdo it, this can make the people in your story feel more real.

she nodded

he bobbed his head

she tilted her head

he cocked his head

she inclined her head

he jerked his head toward...

she threw her head back

he lowered his head

she hung her head

he ducked

she bowed her head

he put his head in his hands

he covered his eyes with a hand

she hid behind her book

she pressed her hands
to her cheeks

she raised her chin

he lifted his chin

her hands squeezed into fists

his hands tightened into fists

she clenched her fists

she balled her fists	he unclenched his fists
her arms remained at her sides	his arms dangled at his sides
he shrugged	she gave a half shrug
he lifted his shoulder in a half shrug	she gave a dismissive wave of her hand
she raised a hand in greeting	he waved
she held up her hands	he lifted his hands
she held up her palms	he threw his hands in the air
she brushed her palms together	he rubbed his hands together
she made a steeple of her fingers	he spread his hands
she gesticulated	she fanned herself
he flapped his hands	he waved his hands
she clapped her hands	he snapped his fingers
she held up a finger	she wagged a finger
he pointed	she gestured with a thumb
he jerked his thumb toward...	she extended her middle finger toward him
he gave her the finger	she flipped him the bird
she gave him the thumbs up	he gave him the okay sign
she flashed a peace sign	she drew a finger across her throat
he twirled a finger next to his temple	she gave a mock salute

he pretended to shoot
himself in the head

she waggled her hips

he thrust his pelvis

he put his hands on his hips

she rested a hand on her hip

she jutted out her hip

she shoved her hands
into her pockets

he jammed his hands
in his pockets

she folded her arms

he crossed his arms
over his chest

she hugged herself

he wrapped his arms
around himself

she rubbed her forearms

she spread her arms wide

he held out his arms

she held out her hand

he extended a hand

he shook his head

she turned her face away

he looked away

his breaths quickened

she panted

she was breathing hard

his chest rose and fell
with rapid breaths

she took in a deep breath

he drew in a long breath

she took in a sharp breath

he gasped

she held her breath

he let out a harsh breath

she exhaled

he blew out his cheeks

she huffed

he sighed

she snorted

she laughed

he giggled

she guffawed

he chuckled

he gave a mirthless laugh

he cackled

he kneaded his shoulder

she tensed her shoulders

she rubbed her temples

she ran her hand
through her hair

he raked his fingers
through his hair

she toyed with a lock of hair

she twirled her hair

she tucked a lock of
hair behind her ear

she shook out her hair

he buried his hands in his hair

he stroked his beard

she tugged at her earlobe

she chewed on a cuticle

she inspected her fingernails

she gave a bitter laugh

she tittered

she rubbed her shoulder

he rolled his shoulders

he massaged the
back of his neck

she rubbed her hands
on her thighs

he threaded a hand
through his hair

he shoved his hair
away from his face

she played with her hair

she wrapped a curl
around her finger

he undid his ponytail

she tossed her hair

she tugged at her hair

he scratched his beard

he bit a nail

she picked at her nails

he plucked at the
cuff of his shirt

she picked lint from her sleeve	he adjusted the lapels of his jacket
she fiddled with her earring	he twisted the ring on his finger
she played with her cell phone	he tugged at his shirt collar
he adjusted his tie	she smoothed down her skirt
she scratched her nose	he scratched his head
she rubbed her forehead	he blotted his forehead with a handkerchief
she slapped her forehead	he smacked his forehead
he facepalmed	she rubbed her eyes
she pinched the bridge of her nose	he held his nose
he slapped a hand over her mouth	she covered her mouth with her hand
he slapped his knee	she pressed her fingers to her lips
he tapped his fingers against his lips	she held her finger up to her lips
he rubbed his chin	she pressed a hand to her throat
she touched her hand to her heart	he pounded his chest
he clutched his chest	he leaned against the wall
she bounced on her toes	he danced in place
she jumped up and down	he tapped his foot

Bryn Donovan

he stomped his foot

her toes curled

she folded her hands in her lap

she drummed her
fingers on the table

he tapped his fingers
on the table

he slammed his hand
on the table

she pounded her fist
on the table

she set her palms down
flat on the table

he rested his hands
on the table

she set her hands on
the table, palms up

he leaned back in his chair

she hooked her feet
around the chair legs

he gripped the arm of the chair

she put her hands
behind her head

he put his feet up on the desk

he fidgeted

she jiggled her foot

he swung his leg

she crossed her legs

he uncrossed his legs

she crossed her ankles
in front of her

she stretched out her
legs in front of her

he sprawled out

she cringed

he shuddered

she flinched

he recoiled

he shivered

she trembled

his body shook

she cowered

he shrank back

she huddled in the corner

he pulled away

she jerked away

he turned away

she stilled	he froze
she jolted upright	he stiffened
she straightened	he tensed
he jumped	she jumped to her feet
he stood up	she rose from her seat
she relaxed	he hunched
she slouched	her shoulders sagged
his shoulders slumped	her shoulders rounded
his chest caved	he drooped
she wilted	he went limp
he rolled his shoulders	she squared her shoulders
she clasped her hands behind her back	he puffed out his chest
she thrust out her chest	he propped his chin on his hand
she rested her chin on her palm	he yawned
she stretched	he turned around
she whirled around	he pivoted
she reeled	he staggered
her knees buckled	she stepped away
she drew nearer	he leaned closer
she inched forward	he loomed closer

Bryn Donovan

he paced

she shifted from one
foot to the other

she rocked back and forth

he shuffled his feet

he swayed on his feet

she dragged her feet

she pumped a fist

he thrust his fists in the air

she punched the air

PHYSICAL DESCRIPTIONS

Sometimes it can be hard to find the right words to describe individual facial features, faces in general, bodies, and even hair. This list can be a good resource for describing the looks of the characters in your story.

Remember that when you're in a character's point of view, his attitude toward someone else's appearance may change over the course of the story as his relationship to that character changes. A classic case in point: Mr. Darcy goes from saying Elizabeth Bennet is "tolerable, but not handsome enough to tempt me," to "one of the handsomest women of my acquaintance." Conversely, the cute guy in Spanish class might not seem cute at all once your young adult heroine figures out he's a jerk.

Some of these phrases on this list are more expected than others, and you can always put your own spin on them.

EYES - GENERAL

large	small	narrow	sharp
squinty	round	wide-set	close-set
deep-set	sunken	bulging	rheumy
protruding	wide	hooded	heavy-lidded
bedroom	bright	sparkling	glittering
flecked	dull	bleary	cloudy
red-rimmed	beady	birdlike	cat-like
jewel-like	steely	hard	fringed with long lashes
with sweeping eyelashes	with thick eyelashes		

Brown is the most common eye color by far. Green is quite rare.

chestnut	chocolate brown	cocoa brown	coffee brown
mocha	mahogany	sepia	sienna brown
mink brown	copper	amber	cognac
whiskey	brandy	honey	tawny
topaz	hazel	obsidian	onyx
coal	raven	midnight	sky blue
sunny blue	cornflower blue	steel blue	ice blue
Arctic blue	glacial blue	crystal blue	cerulean
sapphire	electric blue	azure	lake blue
aquamarine	turquoise	denim blue	storm blue
slate gray	silver	chrome	platinum
pewter	smoky gray	ash gray	concrete gray
dove gray	shark gray	fog gray	gunmetal gray
olive	emerald	leaf green	moss green

EYEBROWS

arched	straight	plucked	sparse
trim	dark	faint	thin
thick	unruly	bushy	heavy

SKIN – COLOR

Descriptions of the skin tones of characters of color can be a sensitive issue, which is hardly surprising, given the course of history. Many people object to comparing skin tones to food. "Coffee" and "chocolate" probably carry the most negativity, and may be the most overused besides. As is so often the case with language, whether one is a part of the group or outside of it makes a big difference.

amber	bronze	cinnamon	copper
dark brown	deep brown	ebony	honey
golden	pale	pallid	pasty
fair	light	creamy	alabaster
ivory	bisque	milky	porcelain
chalky	sallow	olive	peach
rosy	ruddy	florid	russet
tawny	like gingerbread	like strong tea	like weak tea with milk

SKIN – GENERAL

Some of these are better for the face, and some are better for other parts of the body.

lined	wrinkled	seamed	leathery
sagging	drooping	loose	clear
smooth	silken	satiny	dry
flaky	scaly	delicate	thin
translucent	luminescent	baby-soft	flawless
poreless	with large pores	glowing	dewy
dull	velvety	fuzzy	rough
uneven	mottled	dimpled	doughy
firm	freckled	pimply	pockmarked
blemished	pitted	scarred	bruised
veined	scratched	sunburned	weather-beaten
raw	tattooed		

FACE - STRUCTURE

square	round	oblong	oval
elongated	narrow	heart-shaped	catlike
wolfish	high forehead	broad forehead	prominent brow ridge

protruding brow bone	sharp cheekbones	high cheekbones	angular cheekbones
hollow cheeks	square jaw	chiseled	sculpted
craggy	soft	jowly	jutting chin
pointed chin	weak chin	receding chin	double chin
cleft chin	dimple in chin	protruding Adam's apple	

NOSE

snub	dainty	button	turned-up
long	broad	thin	straight
pointed	crooked	aquiline	Roman
bulbous	flared	hawk	strong

MOUTH/LIPS

thin	narrow	full	lush
thick	plump	Cupid's bow	rosebud
dry	cracked	chapped	moist
glossy	straight teeth	crooked teeth	gap between teeth
gleaming white teeth	overbite	underbite	

FACIAL HAIR (OR LACK THEREOF)

clean-shaven	smooth-shaven	beard	neckbeard
goatee	moustache	sideburns	mutton chops
stubble	a few days' growth of beard	five o' clock shadow	

HAIR – GENERAL

long	short	shoulder-length	loose
limp	dull	shiny	glossy
sleek	smooth	luminous	lustrous
spiky	stringy	shaggy	tangled
messy	tousled	windblown	unkempt
bedhead	straggly	neatly combed	parted
slicked down	slicked back	cropped	clipped
buzzed	buzz cut	crewcut	pixie cut
mullet	bob	afro	natural
braids	cornrows	dreadlocks	pigtails
ponytail	bun	updo	bouffant
comb-over	bald	shaved	bushy

frizzy	wavy	curly	straight
lanky	oily	greasy	dry
layers	corkscrews	spirals	ringlets
widow's peak	thick	luxuriant	voluminous
full	wild	untamed	bouncy
fine	thinning		

HAIR – COLOR

black	blue-black	jet black	raven
ebony	inky black	midnight	sable
salt and pepper	silver	charcoal gray	steel gray
white	snow-white	brown	brunette
chocolate brown	coffee brown	ash brown	brown sugar
nut brown	caramel	tawny brown	toffee brown
red	ginger	auburn	Titian-haired
copper	strawberry blonde	butterscotch	honey
wheat	blonde	golden	sandy blond
flaxen	fair-haired	highlighted	bleached

HANDS

delicate	small	large	square
sturdy	strong	smooth	rough
calloused	elegant	plump	manicured
stubby fingers	long fingers	ragged nails	grimy fingernails

BODY

tall	average height	short	petite
tiny	compact	big	large
burly	beefy	bulky	brawny
barrel-chested	heavy	heavyset	fat
overweight	obese	flabby	chunky
chubby	pudgy	pot-bellied	portly
thick	stout	lush	plush
full-figured	ample	rounded	generous
voluptuous	curvy	hourglass	plump
leggy	long-legged	gangling	lanky
coltish	lissome	willowy	lithe
lean	slim	slender	trim
thin	skinny	emaciated	gaunt

bony	spare	solid	stocky
wiry	rangy	sinewy	stringy
ropy	sturdy	strapping	powerful
hulking	fit	athletic	toned
built	muscular	chiseled	taut
ripped	Herculean	broad-shouldered	sloping shoulders
bowlegged			

EMOTIONAL DESCRIPTIONS

As writers, we're always looking for vivid ways to describe emotions. If we only write things like, *He felt sad, she felt angry, he was devastated, she was elated...* the reader won't feel much at all.

We can convey many feelings through facial expressions, body language, and gestures. However, you're limited in how much you can describe the facial expressions of your point-of-view character. She can't see her own face, so you can't go much beyond the occasional "she smiled" or "she could feel herself blushing." And if your character is hiding her emotions, she may be feeling something deeply without conveying it through gestures or body language at all.

This list focuses on two other ways we can make emotions more vivid: assigning an active verb to them, and describing how the emotions physically feel in the body. The latter can be done directly, or you can use metaphorical language to evoke reactions like an adrenaline spike or a dopamine rush. Descriptions of how emotions physically feel should be used judiciously, because they indicate unusually strong feelings, but use them when appropriate because they're a good way to elicit a reader response.

There are, of course, endless ways to describe emotions. If something here feels too familiar, you can always alter it slightly to make it your own.

Please note that you can turn almost any of these into a supporting phrase in your story. For instance, *humiliation overcame her* can become *overcome with humiliation.*

I've focused on some basic, primal emotions: desire, anger, fear, disgust, shame, sadness, and joy. You may find inspiration here for describing other feelings as well.

DESIRE

her knees weakened	his knees turned to water
her knees wobbled	she felt breathless

his breath caught

her breath hitched

he stole her breath

he felt dizzy

her flesh tingled

her skin flushed

warmth spread through her

longing whispered through her

his desire flickered to life

heat curled down her spine

every inch of him craved her

her body sizzled

her heart skittered

his heart thumped

her heart nearly stopped

passion ignited her

she electrified her

desire radiated between them

desire percolated between them

passion took hold of him

heat coursed in his veins

lust blindsided her

his body came to attention

heat pooled in her

his body throbbed

he ached for him

she ached with need

her body begged for his touch

she melted

ANGER

her annoyance flared

he quivered with indignation

his every muscle tensed

her body locked up with rage

rage bottled up inside her

she simmered with anger

he trembled with fury

his blood boiled

anger seared through her

he shook with fury

rage swept over him

her temples throbbed with rage

fury blinded her

anger swelled up in him

flames of anger shot
through her

she choked on her anger

rage flashed through her

her pulse slammed in her neck

anger roared through him

anger rolled through her

his brain exploded with fury

rage poisoned her veins

rage fueled her

fury poured through her

anger crashed through him

anger thundered through him

FEAR

his breath shook

an alarm rang in her mind

his heart pounded

his heart thudded

his heart was in his throat

his chest tightened with fear

worry gnawed at her

fear clawed through her

fear twisted her gut

the pit of her stomach fell

she was barely able to breathe

she bit back a scream

her heart drummed

her chest stuttered

fear splintered his heart

worry snaked through her

anxiety swirled around her

he shivered

his stomach knotted

sweat trickled down his spine

her blood ran cold

it chilled his soul

fear paralyzed her

her mouth turned dry

a chill went through him

fear hit her like icy water

panic assailed him

DISGUST

he battled the urge to recoil

he suppressed a shudder

a wave of nausea hit him

he tasted bile

she gagged

it turned her stomach

his stomach revolted

his stomach churned

his flesh prickled

she forced down a sick feeling

she fought the urge
to throw up

she wanted to puke

bitterness filled her mouth

his gorge rose

her stomach roiled

her stomach heaved

her skin crawled

SHAME

embarrassment stirred in her

embarrassment seized her

his scalp prickled with shame

she cringed inwardly

shame spiraled through him

he burned with humiliation

heat crept into her cheeks

embarrassment racked her

guilt tormented him

guilt consumed her
from within

shame corroded his insides

humiliation overcame her

shame engulfed him

she wanted to curl up in shame

inwardly, he winced

embarrassment coiled
around him

she floundered in
embarrassment

shame washed over him

guilt flooded over her

he wanted to disappear

she wanted to die on the spot

SADNESS

sorrow closed up her throat

his throat clenched

her throat thickened with sobs

his vision blurred

his throat tightened

pain gripped her chest

sadness tore at his chest

her heart wrenched

it felt like a knife to his heart

a weight settled on her heart

he crumbled inside

his mood plummeted

her spirits fell

his hopes disintegrated

he descended into depression

disappointment sagged
through him

it plunged him into despair

she was drowning in her grief

sorrow shredded her insides

his body felt leaden

despair dragged her down

grief hollowed her out

he felt empty inside

sadness crushed him

he could hardly move

she felt numb all over

dejection burdened her

grief shattered him

she felt cold

his bones ached

numbness infused her body

JOY

joy bubbled up in her

joy overwhelmed her

it buoyed her spirits

happiness flowed through her

joy filled him like sunshine

joy warmed him from within

his heart leaped

joy welled up in her heart

joy danced through her heart

happiness bloomed inside her

fresh energy filled him

happiness coursed through her

elation suffused his being

he glowed inside

it lifted her mood

her hopes rose

warmth filled his chest

happiness sparkled inside her

her heart felt light

she got a warm, fuzzy feeling

hope fluttered inside her

her hopes kindled

joy blossomed within her

exultation surged through him

excitement raced through her

she felt fully alive

his spirits soared

he felt light on his feet

he felt giddy

she felt drunk with happiness

she felt weightless

she felt like she was floating

it felt like a caffeine buzz

EVOCATIVE IMAGES

The right visual can carry a real emotional punch. It can serve as foreshadowing or characterization, or it can underscore the impact of the action.

Poetry and film make the most use of evocative images, but many novels hinge upon them as well. Most people who have read F. Scott Fitzgerald's *The Great Gatsby,* for instance, remember the ominous eyes of Doctor T.J. Eckleburg on the billboard, the green light at the end of Daisy's dock, and Gatsby's beautiful multicolored shirts flung out on a table for Daisy's approval.

I almost put this list in the Settings section of the book, but I think strong images are often more about a character's moment of perception than about setting the scene in general. Sometimes focusing in closely on a single image can give the whole scene more impact.

This list contains visuals that I think have the power to resonate in your story. I have separated them into indoor and outdoor images, although technically, many could be either. They are in no particular order, though I've often put similar things next to each other. I hope they will help you think of many more.

INDOOR

An empty classroom.

A baseball glove: child or adult size, new or worn.

A mitten without a match.

A child's shoes.

Children in school uniforms.

A woman in a sundress.

A man in a three-piece suit.

A lady's hat for wearing to church.

A trucker hat.

A flannel shirt.

An unmade bed.

A bedroom plastered with posters.

A pile of dishes in the sink.

Dust particles in the air.

A flickering candle flame.

A diamond ring.

A pocket watch.

A FedEx package.

Flutes of champagne,
with the tiny bubbles
rising to the surface.

A dead houseplant.

A cockroach with
twitching antennae.

A taxidermy animal head,
or the whole animal.

A dirty or naked doll,
or part of one.

A shopping cart.

An old road map.

Skeins of colorful yarn.

A crocheted afghan.

Plastic bins full of stuff, in
the attic or the basement.

The view of a city from the
top of a tall building.

Condensation on a
glass of ice water.

A wedding gown
hung on a door.

A pearl necklace.

A birthday cake.

Party balloons.

A dozen roses.

A spider.

Drops of blood in the sink
or on the bathroom tile.

A human skull, or
a carved one.

A mannequin.

A Halloween or carnival mask.

A desktop globe.

A pincushion full of pins.

A cross-stitched
quote or picture.

Tropical fish in an aquarium.

A spiral notebook full of
notes and scribblings.

A "Help Wanted" sign
in a storefront.

Shag carpeting.

Stained glass windows.

An ice cream cone with
rainbow sprinkles.

A pair of cowboy boots.

Cream swirling in coffee.

A delivery pizza in a
greasy cardboard box.

The glow of an open
refrigerator.

A single eyelash on a
fingertip or cheek.

A box of condoms.

An ashtray full of
cigarette butts.

A row of perfume or
cologne bottles.

Bookcases full of books.

A winding staircase.

A chandelier.

A new box of crayons.

A claw-foot bathtub.

A long row of high
school lockers.

A jar of homemade preserves.

A leather jacket.

An elegant porcelain
teacup and saucer.

Raw steaks or raw hamburger.

A bowl full of M&Ms.

A hairbrush full of hair.

A tampon or sanitary
pad, used or not.

A bra on the floor.

An empty whiskey bottle.

A souvenir snow globe.

A tall ladder.

A ceiling fan.

Piano keys.

A bare mattress.

Tarot cards.

Scrabble tiles.

Suitcases by the door.

An umbrella—brightly
colored or classic black.

A blanket fort.

Dice.

A chessboard and pieces.

Binoculars.

OUTDOOR

Fall leaves swirling
in the wind.

Gnarled tree roots.

An empty stadium.

A reflection of the
sky in a puddle.

Sunglasses reflecting someone
else's face or a landscape.

A dead bird on the pavement.

A police car.

Sunlight streaming
through tree branches.

A bird's nest.

A red cardinal on a
snowy branch.

The skeleton of a
desiccated leaf.

A monarch butterfly, flitting
among weeds and wildflowers.

The reflections of clouds
on the glass windows
of a skyscraper.

A rainbow in an oil slick.

A vacant lot full of weeds.

A fire truck.

Wet city streets at night.

A hornet's nest or beehive.

A single feather.

A flock of birds rising up
and flying away all at once.

A crocus poking out
of the snow.

A cherry tree in blossom.

A field full of sunflowers.

A dandelion ready to
be wished on.

Horses grazing in a pasture.

Haystacks.

A weathered barn.

The framework of a
house being built.

Wind turbines.

Ripples in a pond.

A road shrouded with mist.

A campfire, with sparks
flying upward.

Fireworks.

A house lit up by a zillion
lights for Christmas.

A porch light.

A night light.

The glossy fronds
of palm trees.

Seashells and sand dollars.

Saguaro cacti in the desert
with their arms in the air.

A canyon.

Carousel horses.

A Ferris wheel.

A pile of pumpkins.

Hand-lettered roadside signs.

Jet trails in a blue sky.

Rows of identical
suburban homes.

A swimming pool.

A colorful city mural.

Sprawling graffiti on a wall.

A dumpster.

Smoke pouring from the
smokestacks of a power plant.

An inflated flailing
tube man in front of a
used-car dealership.

Bryn Donovan

Clothes hanging on a line.

A barbed wire fence.

A garden gate.

A mobile home or trailer.

A hammock.

Brightly painted toenails.

Footprints in the
sand or the snow.

A sofa set out on the curb.

A blue bicycle.

A harvest moon.

A bolt of lightning
hitting the earth.

Cars lined up bumper to
bumper on the interstate.

A rowboat.

A suspension bridge.

A castle, intact or in ruins.

A white picket fence.

A rusting wrought iron fence.

An old neon sign for a
motel, diner, or bar.

A camping tent.

Waves crashing into
a rocky shore.

Sand dunes.

A splashing city fountain.

A red wagon.

Iridescent soap bubbles.

A streaking meteor.

A sleek sports car.

A dusty pickup truck.

A metal tackle box or toolbox.

A church steeple.

MAKING METAPHORS

A metaphor is a comparison of something to something else. Some of us had teachers who drilled into our heads that a simile uses "like" or "as," and a metaphor does not, but it's not that important of a distinction. Both make a reader think of something in a new way. It might even stick with her for a long time.

In order to work, the metaphor needs to line up with the point of view and the tone of the story. A funny character's wit may be expressed through the hilarious comparisons she makes in her mind, while poetic metaphors may underscore a soulful narrative.

I didn't create a list of metaphors, since their power comes from their originality. Some writers seem to have a natural gift for creating them, and if you're one of those writers, you probably don't need to be reading this at all.

If creating metaphors doesn't always come automatically to you, though, it's still something you can improve on with practice. I want to share one method that can help you write them. I first used this when I was teaching a beginning poetry workshop at university, and I've shared it with other people since.

First, write down a few concrete images, like *blue jay, geode,* or *gymnasium.* Feel free to use any from the preceding list.

For each of these nouns, write a few adjectives that describe them. For blue jay, I wrote down *vivid* and *argumentative.* It's okay if you write some phrases. For geode, I jotted down *sparkly on the inside.*

Now without thinking about it too much, write down some other things that those adjectives or descriptions can describe.

From this, you should begin to see a good metaphor or two. For instance, for *argumentative,* one of the things I wrote down was *children.* Now I could write something like, "Outside the window, blue jays argued like cranky children." For the geode, I wound up with, "The geode sparkled inside, like a brain full of daydreams."

Some of these will work better than others, and some won't work at all, but it's a good way to get to ideas you might not have come up with otherwise. The more you practice coming up with comparisons, the more they will pop into your head on their own.

If you use clichéd metaphors in your first draft—"cold as ice," "free as a bird"—it doesn't mean *you* are unoriginal. It's normal to think of those familiar phrases first. Just circle each one, give it some thought, and replace it with something fresher when appropriate. It doesn't matter what a first version looks like. It's the final draft that counts.

2. SETTINGS

The setting of a story is often an afterthought, but it has a big impact. The mood of a place can reflect the mood of a scene, or stand in ironic contrast to it. The setting can function almost as part of the supporting cast. An evocative place can even inspire a whole story.

Sometimes when you're feeling apathetic or cranky, getting out of the house and going somewhere new can make all the difference. The same can hold true for your writing. If you're stuck, your scene is falling flat, or your characters are stalled, think outside the house.

An interesting location or the backdrop of a particular event can add more flair to a first encounter, a showdown, or a breakup, breakdown, or breakthrough. Of course, your characters need to have a good reason to be there, but you're clever enough to figure that out. The first list in this section will give you some ideas.

As writers, many of us fall short in describing settings in sensory terms beyond the visual. This is because most of us are more consciously aware of what we see, whereas we often process stimuli like background noises and faint smells on an unconscious level—particularly if they are sounds or smells we encounter over a long period, or every day.

Nonetheless, sound and scent can create a strong sense of place in your story. Appealing to senses beyond the visual will make your readers feel like they're really there.

What's more, noises can have a strong emotional impact on your reader. One of my friends has a child who likes to watch scary movies, but when they get *too* scary, he covers his ears. He figured out that it's less intense without the soundtrack. While we can't impose a soundtrack over a page, we can still evoke sounds to affect the experience. Scent can be even more powerful, speaking to the most primal part of the readers' brains and triggering memories.

To help you incorporate aural and olfactory cues into your scenes, I've made these two lists of ambient sounds and smells. Most of these are contemporary, but I've included some vintage ones as well.

Bryn Donovan

100 POTENTIALLY INTERESTING SETTINGS FOR SCENES

Some of these are merely locations, while others are events. The list of evocative images can suggest additional settings.

1. A coffeehouse.

2. A bar.

3. A church service.

4. A funeral.

5. A wedding.

6. A graduation ceremony.

7. A beauty salon or barbershop.

8. An airport.

9. A hotel.

10. A cruise ship.

11. A forest trail.

12. Under a bridge.

13. Along the side of a highway.

14. The route of a marathon.

15. An office holiday party.

16. A library.

17. A music festival.

18. The department of motor vehicles.

19. A basement.

20. An attic.

21. A Renaissance faire.

22. A cemetery.

23. A beach.

24. A public pool.

25. A lake or a river.

26. A campground.

27. A ball game—Little League, or major league.

28. A stock car race.

29. A hockey game.

30. An abandoned building.

31. A construction site.

32. A rooftop.

33. A parking garage.

34. A dentist's office.

35. A hospital.

36. A psychiatric ward.

37. An assisted living facility.

38. A gym or fitness center.

39. A locker room.

40. A city sidewalk.

41. A museum.

42. A tattoo parlor.

43. A lingerie department.

44. A grocery store.

45. A drugstore.

46. A home improvement store.

47. A giant discount store.

48. A flea market.

49. A farmer's market.

50. A tractor pull.

51. A backyard barbecue.

52. A convenience store.

53. A public restroom.

54. The post office.

55. A cave.

56. A subway.

57. A bus stop.

58. A theater.

59. A movie multiplex.

60. A children's recital or school play.

61. A children's birthday party.

62. A high school prom.

63. A family reunion.

64. A high school or college reunion.

65. A cornfield.

66. A riding stable.

67. A shooting range.

68. A mountaintop.

69. A casino.

70. A morgue.

71. A lighthouse.

72. A costume party.

73. A parade route.

74. A political demonstration.

75. A car dealership.

76. An automotive garage.

77. A courthouse.

78. A city council meeting.

79. A TV news station.

80. A tax office.

81. A bank.

82. A payday loan agency.

83. A thrift store.

84. A diner.

85. A five-star restaurant.

86. An executive boardroom.

87. An animal shelter.

88. A dog park.

89. A playground.

90. A golf course—public, or part of a resort or club.

91. An observatory or planetarium.

92. A food bank or community pantry.

93. A church potluck.

94. An awards dinner.

95. A charity gala event.

96. A laundromat.

97. A greenhouse, gardening center, or plant nursery.

98. A front porch.

99. A winery or a brewery.

100. A dark alley.

SOUNDS FOR SETTINGS

motorcycle engine revving

car motor running

scraping on windshield

seat belt buckle clinking

car door closing

car stereo bass

cars rushing by

cars honking

car crashing

construction equipment

vehicles beeping as they back up

tires or footsteps on gravel

police, fire, or ambulance siren

fire alarm

tornado siren

trains on tracks

helicopters

bicycle wheels spinning

bicycle bell

horseshoes on cobblestones

rattling carriages

factory whistle

buzz saw

chainsaw

hammering

sanding wood

carpenter drill

dentist drill

ice cream truck music

balloon popping

garage door opening

lawn mower

lawn sprinkler

shoveling dirt

weights clanking at a gym

drone of a treadmill

basketball bouncing

squeaky toy

cat purring

dog whining

rooster crowing

crickets chirping

a fly buzzing

bees buzzing

birds chirping

owl hooting

thunder

transformer blowing

train whistle

foghorn

seagulls

flag flapping

leaves crunching underfoot

raking leaves

fireworks

gun cocking

shoes squeaking on a basketball court

cat meowing

dog barking

dog panting

cows mooing

locusts or cicadas droning

a mosquito buzzing

frogs croaking

birds or bats flapping

rain on a roof

lightning strike

trains on tracks

warning bell at a train crossing

ocean waves

whistling wind

wind chimes

snow crunching underfoot

crackling fire

gun loading

gunfire

alarm clock

grandfather clock chiming

dinner bell

buzz of fluorescent lights

typewriter

scissors cutting paper or fabric

radio static

marker squeaking on paper
or a dry erase board

elevator hum

hum of air conditioning
and heating

briefcase clicking shut

airplane taking off or landing

airplane "unfasten
seat belt" bing

phone ringing

dial tone

knock on door

slamming door

TV blaring

clinking pocket change

buzz of conversation

ticking clock

church bells

school bell

typing on keyboard

stapler

sewing machine

microphone feedback

copy machine

elevator ding

announcements over
loudspeakers

backpack or suitcase zipping

airplane bins clicking shut

footsteps in halls

busy signal on an old phone

doorbell

creaking door

breaking glass

clinking of ice in a glass

jingling keys

laughter

cheering

clapping

crying baby

laughing baby

screaming children

coughing

blowing nose

sneezing

snoring

splashing in water

broom sweeping

vacuum cleaner

washer or dryer hum

squeak of cleaning a
window or mirror

bath or shower running

splashing water

dripping faucet

toilet flushing

electric hand dryer

hair dryer

aerosol can spraying

chair scraping on floor

coffee brewing

tea kettle whistling

sizzling oil or bacon

popcorn popping

rustle of potato chip bag

slurping through a straw

aluminum can being crushed

garbage disposal

microwave ding

Styrofoam cooler squeaking

champagne cork popping

SCENTS FOR SETTINGS

There are thousands of food, flower, and plant smells, and I have included many that I think are particularly evocative or seem to carry a long way. Some of these are brand-name items, because their smells are that distinctive. I apologize for the disgusting smells on this list, but I'm sure your characters encounter gross things now and again.

Women in general have a significantly better sense of smell than men do, because they have so many more neurons in the olfactory bulbs in their brains. However, you could certainly write a male character with an acute sense of smell.

gasoline	pool chlorine
freshly mowed grass	wet earth
manure	ozone
salty ocean air	suntan lotion
lilacs	honeysuckle
jasmine	lavender
mint	sugar maple leaves
burning leaves	campfire
peat fire	pine trees
creosote bush	decomposing wood
skunk	mold
must	old asbestos tiles

dusty heating ducts

new textbooks

crayons

tempera paint

Play-Doh

hot pavement

ripe garbage

car exhaust

diesel fumes from buses

cigarette smoke

urine

charred pretzels

fresh coffee

barbecue

fresh-baked bread

movie popcorn

lemon

bacon

cinnamon

cookies baking

roasting chicken or turkey

floor wax

fresh pencil shavings

markers

paste

wet sidewalks

fresh tar

rotting meat

jet fuel

air freshener in cabs

cigar smoke

sewer gas (a rotten egg smell)

hot dog stands

burned coffee

takeout pizza

fast food French fries

ripe peaches

sautéed garlic

toast

curry

chocolate

just-blown-out matches

pipe tobacco	whiskey
beer	marijuana
incense	patchouli
candles	old books
fresh twenty-dollar bills	new carpet
new paint	fresh varnish
new vinyl shower curtain liner	wet dog
litter box	diaper pail
feces	flatulence
sour milk	vomit
new clothing	fresh laundry
dirty laundry	stinky sneakers
Band-Aids	Neosporin
blood	rubbing alcohol
vinegar	Pine-Sol
Fabuloso (cleaner popular in Mexico)	furniture polish
ammonia	bleach
sawdust	fresh lumber
leather	gun oil
bouquet of roses	Chanel No. 5

perfume

Vicks VapoRub

Old Spice

mouthwash

morning breath

body odor

shampoo

hairspray

nail polish remover

wool coat

the top of a baby's head

cold cream

aftershave

deodorant

chewing gum

sweat

soap

hair dye

nail polish

shoe polish

baby powder

puppy breath

3. PLOTTING

You'll notice that all my plot ideas are about conflict. A story is boring without it, not to mention unrealistic. Shakespeare wrote, "The course of true love never did run smooth," and that's true of the course of almost everything else as well.

The right plot, of course, depends on your character. Let's say you have a story about someone who is compelled to spend a week at a nudist resort. That may not be a very interesting story if it stars a free-spirited bohemian type, but it's great for a conservative, modest character. You want the storyline to introduce obstacles that make people have to struggle, change, and grow.

Although I adore stories about friendship, I didn't make a separate category for it, because there are many storylines in the other sections that can be used for friends, too.

Some of the ideas here are more specific than others. However, every single one is so skeletal that it could be handled in countless different ways. They aren't entire plots, just thought starters, and the way you develop them is what will make them great.

50 ROMANCE PLOTS

Romance plots aren't just for romance novels. They are often central to young adult novels, literary novels, movie scripts, and even fantasy novels. Frequently, romance provides a subplot for other genres of storytelling as well. Love is complicated, and you might use more than one of these story ideas in your next work.

As you read these, please remember that the pronouns are just placeholders, and you can cast people of any gender or no particular gender into any role.

1. She's already ruled him out—she made up her mind a long time ago that she would only marry a doctor, or she would *never* date a biker again.

2. They are competitors for the same job or the same championship.

3. They are straight-up enemies. He wants to buy the land to build a resort, and she wants to see it turned into a nature sanctuary. He's the defense attorney, and she's the prosecutor. They're soldiers on opposing sides of the war... the possibilities are endless here!

4. He already won...he inherited an estate that should have been hers, or he got the job that she was hoping to be promoted into, and she's seething.

5. He broke her heart in the past. Maybe there was a good reason behind it, or maybe he was an idiot then and realizes it now. It's possible he just *ignored* her.

6. She did our heroine wrong in the past, or maybe she wronged the heroine's family member or friend.

7. He did something wrong in the past, period. Although she wasn't the victim, it was really bad. How can she be sure he's changed?

8. She has trust issues, because her last relationship ended in a terrible betrayal.

9. He has intimacy issues. Maybe because of a traumatic past, he feels too vulnerable if anyone knows about his real emotions or weaknesses. Maybe she's a psychic, a behavioral expert, or just the one person who can see right through him... and it makes him uncomfortable as hell.

10. She doesn't want to be in a relationship at all. She's taken a break from dating, or she vowed to never get tied down.

11. She believes no one can truly love her. Perhaps she made a terrible mistake in the past, or she's not attractive in the conventional manner, or she's a "fallen woman" in a repressive era.

12. They are good friends, and they don't want to risk ruining their friendship by taking it to the next level.

13. They are co-workers, and they don't want to make things weird at the office, bar, or school where they both work.

14. He has a secret. He might be in a witness protection program, for instance, or he might have an undisclosed medical condition.

15. She's freaked out by who he really is—a werewolf, ex-con, or a funeral director.

16. It was supposed to be sex only. They were going to be friends with benefits, or maybe he's a male escort. Falling in love goes against the original arrangement.

17. Their love was supposed to be fake. They were pretending to be in love or married, or they entered a marriage of convenience. It can't be real, can it? On a related note...

18. He was faking it at first. Maybe he made a bet that he could bed her, or he pretended to like her so he could learn her secrets and be the journalist who broke the story.

19. She was stuck with him. He's a partner on a job she wanted to do by herself, or he rescued her when she was actually pretty happy where she was. She doesn't want to admit she's actually falling for him.

20. He has moral qualms about getting into a relationship. He might be her teacher, her captor, or her employer. Alternatively, maybe she's his best friend's ex, and that gives him pause.

21. She's a mess. She's grieving the death of her husband, partner, or child, or she has PTSD from battle or being kidnapped.

22. He has a mental illness or addiction that causes problems in the relationship.

23. Their love is forbidden by others. It's against the rules, spoken or unspoken, of their family, organization, community, nation, or religion.

24. Our hero isn't sure if he wants to risk making a move, because the guy he likes might not be gay.

25. Our heroine is confused, because she thought she liked guys, but now she's crushing on a girl.

26. Their cultures clash. It could be that he's a modern man and she's from ancient Greece, or she's a big-city girl and he's a small-town boy. This may overlap with the next one.

27. They are from different social classes.

28. One of them is promised to someone else. The wedding might already be planned. She might have reasons for going through with a loveless or lackluster marriage.

29. One of them is actually married to someone else. It might be legitimate. On the other hand, maybe it is some weird legal, not-consummated arrangement, or maybe her husband is an abusive monster.

30. She is infatuated with someone else instead of our hero. It may be that she doesn't realize yet that this other person is awful.

31. She is interested in someone else in addition to our hero, and she's having trouble making a decision. Maybe she refuses to choose.

32. Their time together is limited. Possibly she's going abroad to study in the fall, his work visa is almost up, or she's about to go on a space mission to another planet, never to return. What's the point of getting serious?

33. Being together would require a big sacrifice. She would have to say no to her dream job, or he would have to live in New York City when his cowboy heart loves the Montana skies.

34. He's a danger to her safety. Maybe he's a vampire, or maybe he has enemies in the mafia.

35. She thinks she'll only make him unhappy, because she's dying of a disease, suffering under a curse, or can't have children. (Note that in many cases, this conflict may be exaggerated in the character's mind.)

36. He's ugly, freaky, or scary-looking.

37. She's disguised as someone he would never fall for... a man when he's only into women, or a conservative when he's a die-hard liberal.

38. She may or may not be real at all. Maybe he is being catfished, or maybe he is meeting a fairy or alien in his dreams.

39. They can't get together in real life. There may be an ocean or a few centuries between them.

40. He is a suspect in a criminal investigation.

41. They have terrible first impressions of one another, and it's hard to admit they were wrong. They might have gotten off to an awful start by arguing about something.

42. Her family is the problem. Maybe they are obnoxious or immoral, and he doesn't want to get involved with that. Alternately, maybe she has a couple of kids, and while they are cute, this is not what he imagined for himself.

43. He has a reputation... as a heartless womanizer, a stone cold killer, or a greedy corporate lawyer.

44. She doesn't want distractions. She has one very important job to do, and she can't afford to get sidetracked.

45. He loves her, but she doesn't know him. Maybe he knows her from an alternate universe, or maybe she has amnesia.

46. He is too controlling, because he's trying to protect her. Maybe he doesn't want her to be ostracized by Victorian society or to be in danger by becoming a firefighter.

47. He doesn't see her in a romantic way. For instance, she might be the younger sister of his best friend, and he still thinks of her as a kid.

48. They were lovers before, and it ended. Would it be crazy to try again? Would he take her back?

49. The job is getting in the way. It's hard to be romantic when you're working day and night on a political campaign or helping fellow victims of the airplane crash survive in the mountains.

50. Their personalities clash. Maybe he's driven, while she's very laid-back. Maybe he's an eternal optimist and she's a pessimist, so they get on each other's nerves. They will have to meet in the middle, or at least accept one another, in order to make it work.

50 HIGH-STAKES PLOTS

For suspense, thriller, mystery, and action-adventure stories, you want intense, life-or-death plots. Many other genres, such as science fiction, fantasy, horror, romantic suspense, and paranormal romance, often employ these kinds of story lines as well.

Remember that although we usually think of the heroes as the ones staying within the boundaries of the law and the villains as the ones operating outside it, that's not always the case. And of course, almost every villain is the hero in his own mind. Some of these stories may overlap a little in your next exciting project!

1. Someone wants to destroy the country, planet, or neighborhood and must be stopped.

2. Someone close to the heroine mysteriously disappears.

3. The protagonist, someone he loves, or a team member is kidnapped or taken prisoner and must be recovered.

4. Someone is trying to murder the hero or someone he loves, and he doesn't know why. He might or might not know who it is.

5. Someone is trying to murder the heroine or someone she loves, and she knows exactly why. Maybe the would-be killer has an old grudge, or maybe our heroine has secret information.

6. There's a serial killer on the loose who must be stopped. It could be a person or a monster.

7. A friend or family member has been brainwashed or possessed and has turned into a killer.

8. The heroine, or a group, is escaping prison, slavery, or another kind of oppression.

9. Investigating a loved one's murder leads our hero to a foreign country or into a dangerous underworld.

10. People in a house or building have been taken hostage.

11. A person who has only imagined or played at being a warrior or hero now finds himself in a real battle or a game with big stakes.

12. Someone is lost or stranded in an enemy environment, a harsh wilderness, or some other place where survival is a challenge.

13. A natural or human-made disaster threatens to wipe out our heroine along with everyone else.

14. Someone is resolved to get revenge against the one who ruined his life or the life of a loved one—or at least bring the villain to justice.

15. Our hero is sure someone has been wrongfully accused or convicted of a crime and searches for the real culprit.

16. A community asks a stranger to help save them from outlaws, a dragon, or an alien invasion.

17. The hero is on the run from the law. He may be guilty or he may have been framed.

18. Someone must find, retrieve, or get rid of a magical, cursed, or dangerous object.

19. An ordinary person learns she has special powers that she must quickly learn how to control.

20. The hero has special powers or secret knowledge he must hide, or else risk getting killed.

21. Someone is stealing something significant, such as a priceless painting or a huge amount of money.

22. Someone wound up in the possession of something valuable, dangerous, or important, which leads to trouble.

23. Rivals, enemies, or just seemingly incompatible people join together to take down a bad guy or rescue a mutual friend.

24. A hero is unwillingly turned into a threat—a bomb gets surgically planted in him, he is turned into a zombie, or he's carrying a deadly virus.

25. A criminal is recruited by the good guys so he can bring his unique knowledge or skills to an assignment or case.

26. A team is on a dangerous mission, but a personal conflict between two or more members poses the largest threat.

27. Lovers, brothers, or friends are pitted against one another, and only one of them can survive.

28. Through technology or magical means, someone's identity is wiped out or assumed by another person.

29. A spy, soldier, or assassin decides to help his target instead.

30. A spy or soldier falls in love with the enemy—but remains loyal to her duties.

31. A damaging secret letter or video is made public, and the heroine must deal with the aftermath.

32. A voyeur or fan becomes obsessed, with shocking consequences.

33. A person must travel to a certain point by a certain time—maybe with a prisoner or a treasure in tow—or there will be dire consequences.

34. A human-made creature becomes a deadly threat.

35. A plane, ship, bus, or train crashes or seems likely to crash.

36. Someone turns on his own organization once he discovers that they are actually evil.

37. Through training and determination, an unskilled person becomes an effective soldier, spy, or hero.

38. Someone with a violent past, or someone retiring from a dangerous career, gets pulled back into the fray again.

39. A person in the wrong place at the wrong time becomes an accessory or a witness to a terrible crime.

40. Someone appears to have killed herself, but our heroine is positive it was actually a murder.

41. A small group of people defend themselves against an attack by a much bigger or more powerful force.

42. Hundreds or millions of people are under attack by a small group, possibly via computer viruses or biological weapons.

43. A conspiracy theorist or psychic predicts something awful, but can't get anyone to believe him.

44. The heroine, or a group, wants to overthrow a government or other authorities.

45. Strange events lead our hero to believe that everyone in this seemingly nice family, company, or town is actually hiding some horrific secret.

46. Our heroine is a spy or imposter who has infiltrated a group, and they'll kill her if they discover her true identity.

47. A murder case has been cold for years...and suddenly, a new murder looks like it was committed by that same unknown suspect.

48. The hero must perform a difficult task or do something immoral, or else he or someone he loves will suffer.

49. The heroine must deliberately give up her own life in order to save the lives of others.

50. The hero must kill someone he cares about, or at least let that person die, in order to save a larger group of people.

50 FAMILY PLOTS

In a lot of mainstream fiction, young adult novels, scripts, and plays, family drama is front and center. It also might be a B story in your project, or a backstory for just about any character. A couple of these overlap with the romance plot ideas, but they play out quite differently within a family.

1. A family member is perpetually needy and manipulative, and now he has gone too far.

2. Someone in the family (not necessarily the parent) is emotionally or physically abusive.

3. A family member is having an extramarital affair...or at least, it sure looks that way.

4. She's divorced...and the kids prefer the stepmom.

5. He's their new stepdad...but the kids won't give him a chance.

6. Someone in the family has a mental health issue such as depression, addiction, obsessive-compulsive disorder, hoarding, or post-traumatic stress disorder, and this affects the others.

7. Someone in the family is just plain eccentric, and in certain situations, it's embarrassing.

8. Someone is dying...of cancer, a brain tumor, or another disease. A family member has unresolved issues with the person, or alternately, she doesn't know how she's going to go on without him.

9. Someone has already died...and the family is struggling to deal with it.

10. A family member is a criminal of some kind. Maybe everyone finds out immediately, or maybe he kept it secret for years.

11. Everybody in the family is a criminal, which causes all kinds of complications.

12. One family member, willingly or unwillingly, suffers punishment for another's misdeed.

13. Someone has converted to a new religion, joined a different political party, refused to work at the family business, or broken ranks in some other way that has the rest of the family upset.

14. A family member makes dramatic personal changes, and it's hard for the family to reconcile this with the person they once knew.

15. The parents are on the brink of divorce, and the kids (who may be adults) aren't dealing with it well.

16. The family faces financial difficulty: someone has lost her job, or the family business is dwindling.

17. A family member has a mental, physical, or learning disability that poses challenges for other family members as well.

18. The family has moved to a very different community or country from the one they were used to, and they are all struggling to fit in and feel at home.

19. Someone is pregnant, and others in the family disapprove... perhaps because she's a teenager, a single woman over forty, or has eight kids already.

20. Someone is *not* pregnant, and it's a problem. Maybe the couple's been trying for years. On the other hand, maybe they don't want kids, but their parents want to be grandparents.

21. Someone hid a pregnancy in the past, and now there's a half-sibling or grandchild who nobody knew about until now.

22. A person tracks down her birth mother, or the birth mother tracks down her (possibly adult) child.

23. A parent expects his child to be perfect and/or achieve amazing things, even if this is unrealistic.

24. A parent is over-protective of a child, which leads to conflicts between them or with others.

25. A child is becoming an adult—and a parent or guardian can't deal with it.

26. A child refuses to grow up—and it's making the parent or guardian despair.

27. A family member resents doing more than her share of the work. She might be doing all the housework even though she has a full-time job, or she might be the only one taking care of her aging parent even though her siblings live in town.

28. Someone is doing something risky—enlisting to go to war, for example—and a parent or someone else in the family is against it.

29. Someone has abandoned the family...or at least it feels like it. This could be literal abandonment, or it could just be long days at the office.

30. A family member was estranged because she behaved deplorably in the past, but now she wants reconciliation.

31. The whole family or a few members are on a journey or quest and meet up with obstacles along the way.

32. The stresses of long hours at a job, parenting, and caretaking are pushing one or more family members to the breaking point.

33. The family members are separated against their wishes, perhaps by war, financial necessity, or for legal reasons.

34. They have a visitor or house guest, invited or not, who poses challenges. (Note that this is the plot of many ghost stories.)

35. Members of the family are in a legal battle over something, such as the custody of a child or the settlement of a will.

36. Members of the family are in a physical battle—on opposite sides of a war, or in opposite corners of a boxing ring.

37. A family member has an interest or activity that other people in the family disapprove of—or they would, if they knew about it.

38. One family member, likely a sibling, is jealous of the other, because of her relationship, wealth, success, attractiveness, children, or some combination of the above.

39. Two or more siblings are leaving the other one out of discussions, get-togethers, or even group vacations.

40. A gathering of the extended family brings up old tensions and/or new revelations.

41. The high expectations of an occasion, such as Christmas or a wedding, lead to stress and conflict.

42. A lack of communication in the family has led to a huge misunderstanding.

43. Family members disagree about whether to keep or sell a home, land, or a business.

44. Someone is getting married to a person that nobody else in the family can stand.

45. The families of an engaged couple meet for the first time, and it doesn't go well—either because they are very different, or because some of the family members already have a history.

46. Two people in the family are in love with the same person.

47. Two people in the family are in love with and/or having sex with one another.

48. Parents refuse to have anything to do with their child because they disapprove of his lifestyle...or the child breaks things off with the parents, because he disapproves of them.

49. One family member loans a lot of money to another, who may not be able to pay it back after all.

50. The parents die, and one sibling has to take on the role of a parent.

---

25 WORKPLACE PLOTS

Not very many novels and scripts focus on the workplace, but workplace conflicts are a common subplot in all kinds of stories. Many of the conflicts here involve chain of command and teamwork, which make them appropriate for school stories and war stories as well.

1. A boss or employee is incompetent, stupid, rash, or lacks social skills.

2. Someone in a position of power is too demanding or just plain malicious and bullies subordinates.

3. The new person is different. Because of her gender, race, previous experience, or some other factor, she is ostracized or sabotaged.

4. The new boss is very young and/or inexperienced. No one trusts or respects her.

5. The new person has lied about his experience, and actually has no idea what he is doing.

6. The company is facing layoffs, which is freaking everyone out.

7. A person or team has been given a seemingly impossible assignment.

8. New procedures make it almost impossible to get even ordinary work done.

9. The work itself is so difficult, unpleasant, time-consuming, or dangerous that it's ruining people's lives.

10. Someone is asked to behave unethically in his job for the company's benefit.

11. Someone knows about her company's immoral actions. She either blows the whistle or debates whether she should.

12. Someone has behaved unethically in her job, and now it looks like she could be caught.

13. Someone is accused, rightly or wrongly, of behaving unethically or making a huge mistake, and he faces big consequences.

14. Family obligations, illness, addiction, or another factor makes it almost impossible for someone to meet the demands of the job.

15. A dramatic rumor, true or untrue, causes conflict among the staff.

16. A shocking or embarrassing secret about an employee becomes known to her co-workers.

17. An affair or a wanted or unwanted flirtation is disruptive to the team.

18. A romantic liaison between co-workers ends badly, causing problems.

19. Two co-workers are competing for the same promotion or plum assignment.

20. Two people vie for control over a group project.

21. Someone on the team isn't pulling his own weight. He hardly does any work, and he's getting away with it.

22. An employee is difficult to be around, perhaps because of her negative attitude, inane chatter, or poor hygiene.

23. Something's been stolen—someone's sandwich, office equipment, or sensitive files. It looks like an inside job, but nobody knows who did it.

24. Someone gets caught bad-mouthing a co-worker or superior. For instance, she accidentally sends a scathing email to the wrong person.

25. Someone takes all the credit for another person's work. Maybe he presents her ideas as his own.

25 PLOT TWISTS

Unexpected turns and dramatic reveals are one of the great pleasures of novels and movies. They are the reason why some people hate spoilers.

A well-executed plot twist can keep readers riveted. When they didn't know it was coming but then look back and realize there were hints all along, it's really satisfying. Here are some classic plot twists for you to consider!

1. Someone who was presumed dead is still alive. In a supernatural or speculative story, he may have actually died and been resurrected.

2. Someone who was acting like an enemy reveals herself as an ally.

3. A trusted ally turns out to be an enemy.

4. A seemingly average and ordinary character reveals himself to be a genius, fabulously rich, or in possession of remarkable skills.

5. A character is actually a ghost or a figment of an unstable imagination.

6. The protagonist's entire reality is fake. It's a creation of someone in power, an alternate dimension, or his own extended hallucination.

7. A beloved character suddenly dies or is killed.

8. Someone murders or ruins the person who wronged him, long after it had seemed that he had forgiven the person.

9. A character unexpectedly seduces someone—possibly someone he has no business seducing.

10. Two characters that no one would have ever suspected have been sleeping together all along.

11. Two characters are revealed to be siblings, or parent and child. Depending on how these characters have been interacting, it may be a happy or a disturbing revelation.

12. Someone suddenly remembers his true identity.

13. Everyone finds out that a character has been possessed or controlled by some other person or entity.

14. The outlandish thing a "crazy" person kept insisting was real? It's real.

15. The person who thinks he is the con man is actually being conned.

16. Someone has a twin or a clone.

17. An investigator of a murder, or an assistant to the investigation, is the murderer.

18. The main problem is revealed to be just part of a much bigger and more horrible problem.

19. Some small concern or aberration that nobody paid much attention to turns out to be the biggest problem of all.

20. Someone's attempt to solve a problem winds up making it ten times worse.

21. A character faces a difficult moral choice—and decides to do the wrong thing.

22. A victory is so costly that it seems to set someone up for a final defeat.

23. Each character has double-crossed the other.

24. In his efforts to prevent something awful, someone actually helps it happen.

25. The whole story turns out to be a prequel to a movie or book that came before.

25 PLOT POINTS THAT CAN CRACK READERS UP

Humor is one of the most difficult things to write—a fact generally ignored by prestigious film, television, and book awards. People sometimes think that funny writing is an innate talent, and you either have it or you don't. While some writers have a natural gift for comedy, it's something you can practice and become competent at, just like most skills.

People often laugh when their expectations are subverted. There is something innately optimistic about this kind of humor, because it suggests that our lives are filled with more possibilities than we had considered.

With several of these situations, whether it's funny or not is a matter of degree, just as it is in real life. A little teasing may be amusing, while a cutting remark is just plain mean. A tiny failure may be funny, while a huge one is tragic.

Of course, it all depends on your treatment, but here are some situations likely to make your readers laugh.

1. A character mistakes one person for another.

2. Someone misunderstands her immediate situation, which makes her behavior completely inappropriate. For instance, she believes she's on a first date with a cute guy, when it's actually a job interview.

3. A character is extremely proud or thrilled about something that most people would not feel that proud or thrilled about.

4. Someone is horrified by a situation or an aspect of another person that most people would appreciate.

5. Someone's wacky scheme is not playing out as he had hoped.

6. Someone is going along with an activity that is way out of her comfort zone.

7. After expecting to hate an activity, a character winds up totally getting into it.

8. Someone's attempt to lie his way out of trouble fails and makes things more complicated.

9. A nervous character keeps misspeaking and makes an ass of herself.

10. Under the influence of alcohol or medication, a usually reserved character is goofy or otherwise lets his guard down.

11. Someone who no one expects to be sassy and/or a badass is sassy and/or a badass.

12. A crass or free-spirited character socializes with refined or repressed people.

13. Someone puts an incredible amount of thought and effort into something that most people would consider no big deal.

14. A planned event or performance is a disaster, or just comically underwhelming.

15. A series of small things go ridiculously wrong for the character as she tries to accomplish a basic objective, such as get ready for work, drive to work, or give a presentation.

16. Someone tough is revealed to be a total softie in some way that nobody knew about.

17. A character uses an object, a service, or a public or private space for a very different purpose than what it was created for.

18. Someone is pretending everything is fine, even though something has gone outrageously wrong.

19. A character keeps insisting that something doesn't bother her, but makes it abundantly clear that it does.

20. Intentionally or unintentionally, someone embarrasses her friend by sharing or inventing mildly embarrassing information about him or his past.

21. Two people who can't stand each other or are irritated with one another have to pretend to be in love.

22. An undemonstrative person has to deal with a very affectionate one.

23. Someone witnesses something he would have preferred to never see.

24. A character treats a serious situation in a playful way.

25. Someone breaks the rules in a spectacular fashion.

10 PLOT POINTS THAT CAN
MELT READERS' HEARTS

It's not hard to think of tragedies and losses that will break your readers' hearts. If you want to make readers cry in a good way, however, something here might do it.

1. Someone forgives a penitent person for a big transgression.

2. A character or team with significant limitations or challenges finally triumphs.

3. A person (or a dog) nearly dies but makes a recovery or gets a reprieve.

4. Someone finally confesses his love—or two people finally admit it to each other.

5. A character gets a large or meaningful gift, or a touching letter (or a bunch of them), from a person who died or is separated from her.

6. Someone helps heal another person's long-buried hurt or grief.

7. A misfit or an overlooked character is accepted or recognized by an individual or a group.

8. A character chooses to take a heroic action that seems fated to ruin him.

9. Someone makes a grand gesture of love that makes her vulnerable.

10. Two people who love each other and have been separated for a long time are finally reunited.

50 GOALS AND ASPIRATIONS

One of the simplest ways to craft a story is to give your character a clear goal, put obstacles in the way of this goal, and watch her struggle. Your protagonist may eventually succeed or fail, or she may discover something better than her original vision along the way.

On the other hand, dramatic events in the story may supersede your character's goals. Some goals and aspirations may not fuel the story, but may help show who the character is and what he values.

So what do the people in your story really want? Many of the ideas here are very widespread aspirations. And hey, if you wind up getting ideas for your own bucket list, no extra charge.

1. Find a job.

   She may be out of work, or she may just be stuck in a job she hates.

2. Find a partner.

   Depending on his age, his history, and his comfort with commitment, he might be looking for a husband, or he might just be looking for a boyfriend. In some eras and some situations, love may have nothing to do with your character seeking a spouse.

3. Get a divorce.

   It's not always easy for people to get out of unhappy marriages.

4. Have a baby.

   This common goal could be thwarted by many factors, including the lack of a willing partner, economic challenges, age, health issues, and infertility.

5. Adopt a dog or cat from a shelter.

   This is a little like a very light version of #4. Your character's living situation may be an obstacle, however.

6. Earn a degree or certification.

   Graduating from high school, a vocational school, college, or grad school is a very relatable goal.

7. Travel to a particular destination.

   It could be somewhere in his own country or a foreign nation.

8. Buy a house.

   This might be your character's first house, or one she feels compelled to own for some reason.

9. Run his own business.

   Many people dream of striking out on their own. Maybe your protagonist dreams of it, too.

10. Hang on to her business.

    In tough economic times, a person might be focused on keeping her bridal shop, ranch, or online store afloat.

11. Give up an addiction—drinking, smoking, gambling, or drugs.

    This is a really difficult goal for most, though it can be done.

12. Win a competition.

    It could be a basketball tournament, a Miss Utah pageant, or a chili cook-off.

13. Lose weight.

    This may be the most ubiquitous goal there is.

14. Become strong and muscular.

    This sometimes goes along with #13.

15. Run a 5K, a half marathon, or a marathon.

    This is a popular fitness goal.

16. Recover from a disease, injury, or illness.

    Your character may be undergoing treatment for cancer, or she may be battling a mental illness.

17. Reconcile with someone.

    Your protagonist may want to patch things up with a spouse, girlfriend, or former best friend.

18. Repair something.

    Fixing up an old house is a worthy long-term goal for your character, and fixing up a boat or car is a great goal for a short story.

19. Help someone else thrive.

    A character might want to find the right school for her child with special needs, or find a compatible kidney donor for his spouse. Alternately, she may be trying to fix someone who isn't really trying to fix himself. (Spoiler: it doesn't work.)

20. Have sex—or have better sex.

    Some people are actively seeking to lose their v-card. Others have problems they want to fix in the bedroom.

21. Attend an exciting event.

    Examples include seeing his favorite rock band in concert, going to the Super Bowl, and celebrating New Year's Eve in New York's Times Square. It could also be something personal, such as the birth of his child, if he has challenges in getting there.

22. Ensure an exciting event that she is organizing goes well.

    This could be Christmas with the whole family, a wedding, a family reunion, or a town festival or professional conference she's pulling together.

23. Avoid arrest.

If your character has broken the law, this may be his primary aspiration.

24. Get out of debt.

For someone burdened with a lot of student loans or gambling debts, this may be goal #1.

25. Raise money for a cause.

He may have come up with any number of ways to help a cause he believes in or a person he knows who has fallen on hard times.

26. Change the law.

She may be protesting an unfair rule at her high school or a legal loophole that allows industries to pollute the environment.

27. Convert people.

He may be trying to persuade people to become Christians, vegans, or political conservatives.

28. Move to a better place.

Your character may believe that there's a state, city, or country where she would be much happier.

29. Become popular, or just make some friends.

This might involve attempts to overcome shyness, joining a group or two... or making changes to how he presents himself, which may or may not be wise.

30. Be a better parent.

She may want to spend more quality time with her kids, or stop getting so upset with them.

31. Be her true self.

She may be a transgender person who wants to come out and start living as a woman, or she may want to embrace some other aspect of herself that she's denied.

32. Get a promotion.

He may want his boss's job, or for that matter, he may want to run the whole operation.

33. Learn a foreign language.

This frequently appears on people's lists of things they hope to do someday.

34. Learn how to play a musical instrument.

The piano and the guitar are probably the most popular ones.

35. Learn another new skill or craft.

It could be sword fighting or website development.

36. Read more books.

Here's another "never stop learning" type goal. Some people set a goal of reading a certain number of books per year.

37. Have a weekly "date night" with his spouse.

This is a popular resolution for couples, particularly those with children.

38. Climb a mountain.

Because it's there! As a variation, your character might want to hike somewhere famous, such as the Appalachian Trail, or sail to Australia.

39. See her child get married and have children.

Many parents of adult children desire this, and some of them try hard to make it happen.

40. Create something significant.

Your character might want to make a homemade quilt or a short film.

41. Become famous.

Different people have different ideas about how they might want to make this happen.

42. Be an extra on a television show or a movie.

This is for people who would be happy to be a *little* famous, and who just think that this sounds like fun.

43. Retire.

Although he may want to do it, financial considerations or nervousness about what he'll do all day may be preventing him from making the decision.

44. Own her dream car.

45. Sleep under the stars.

Some people want to do this during a meteor shower. The next one is a similar goal.

46. See the Northern Lights.

47. Get a fantastic tattoo.

A short-term goal, to be sure, but one shared by many.

48. Get organized and get rid of all the clutter.

This usually pertains to a person's own space, but it can also involve the home of an aging or deceased loved one.

49. Sell something.

It could be a house, a car, a screenplay, or a piece of jewelry.

50. Attain spiritual enlightenment.

This may involve your character practicing his faith more fully, or it may mean a quest for answers or for the right path. It may involve travel.

25 MOTIVES FOR MURDER

For your thriller or mystery to ring true, your killer needs to have a reason for doing what he does. A motive will also enable the good guys to catch him. There are lots of reasons why people kill. Some killers may have more than one motive, and some of these motives work for serial killers.

This list may seem morbid, but hey, we writers sometimes need these things! There's a reason why we hope nobody looks at our browser histories, right?

1. A physical fight turns deadly. Either the killer loses control, or she accidentally inflicts more damage than she intended.

2. The murderer kills the victim in order to steal from her.

3. The victim of a robbery or rape puts up a fight, and the struggle ends in his death.

4. The victim was the witness to a crime.

5. A spouse or child murders the victim to claim the insurance money or to inherit the estate.

6. The victim is murdered by a spouse or family member who is sick of his verbal or physical abuse.

7. A spouse wants out of a marriage, but he doesn't want to pay alimony, or have others think he was a bad person. He commits the murder as a means of "instant divorce."

8. The murderer kills his mistress or girlfriend because she is pregnant. Maybe he is married to another woman and doesn't want his wife to find out about the affair, or maybe he doesn't want to be burdened with a child.

9. The killer wants to eliminate his rival in romance, politics, or some other competition.

10. The killer believes the victim personally wronged her—by ridiculing her, firing her, ending their friendship, or "stealing" her man. Note that this grudge might go way back. Also, the supposed injustice may be all in the killer's imagination.

11. The victim personally wronged someone the killer loved. He might have raped the killer's sister, for instance, or financially ruined the killer's father. The killer might be exacting justice after the legal system failed to do so.

12. A boyfriend or husband murders the victim after flying into a jealous rage over a real or suspected infidelity.

13. The victim reminds the murderer of someone who rejected him.

14. The killer gets sexually aroused by murdering women or men to whom he is attracted.

15. In the murderer's mind, she is doing the victim a favor by killing him—because he is suffering on earth, or because he's bound for eternal bliss.

16. The murderer hates the victim's politics, religion, sexual orientation, or ethnicity. He may see himself as a crusader.

17. The killer believes the victim is possessed by a demon. Note that if you are writing a horror or paranormal story, the killer may be correct.

18. The murder is a result of a drug deal gone bad.

19. The guilty party murders his wife or child so that people will feel sorry for his loss.

20. The killer feels inferior, and the murder makes him feel powerful and important.

21. The killer commits a murder in order to frame someone close to the victim and destroy that person's life.

22. The victim's life seems perfect—and the murderer is obsessed with the unfairness of this.

23. A spouse, parent, or child murders a family member because he requires an extraordinary amount of caretaking.

24. The murderer actually mistakes the victim for his real intended target.

25. The killer is an amoral monster who wants to know what it feels like to kill somebody.

25 REASONS TO MOVE TO A NEW TOWN

Leo Tolstoy once said, "All great literature is one of two stories; a man goes on a journey or a stranger comes to town." I don't know if this is true, but there are many wonderful books and movies about these two things. That's why I created a list of reasons to move to a new town, and you could also write about the journey there.

1. She's going to college in this new town, or she might be a foreign exchange student.

2. He just landed a new job there, or his company transferred him to this office. Maybe he thinks it will be a nice place to live. On the other hand, maybe he thinks the town is a dump, but he has no other prospects.

3. Her fiancé or husband got a job there. Maybe they arrive together, or maybe they have been doing the long-distance thing for a while.

4. He's looking for a new job. If you want to work in his field, this is the place to be.

5. She thinks this town is the perfect place to start her bed and breakfast, coffee shop, or other dream business.

6. Even though she's from a small town, she's always dreamed of life in the big city.

7. Even though he was born and raised in a bustling metropolis, he's always fantasized about an idyllic life in the country.

8. His aging parents live there, and he's moving close by so he can look after them.

9. Her siblings or parents live there, and she's a single parent who could use their help with the kids.

10. Her sister's or daughter's family lives there, and she wants to be a part of the kids' lives.

11. He wants to get as far away from his family as possible, because they are unbearable.

12. Her parents died, and she is moving back to her hometown to get the house ready for sale—or maybe live in it.

13. He moved after a terrible scandal or a crime. Maybe he even changed his name.

14. She moved after a painful breakup. There's no avoiding her ex in that little town!

15. Something awful happened to him and he wants to put all those terrible memories behind him.

16. She thinks this is a better place to raise her kids.

17. She's sick of living in a cramped apartment and wants to move to a place with a lower cost of living where she can afford a house.

18. He feels as though he will never meet the woman of his dreams in that tiny hometown—or in that snobbish suburb.

19. She's had it with winter. She was made for this sunny climate.

20. He won't be there forever, but has a work assignment —an environmental study, a consulting gig, or a political campaign to run.

21. She won't be there forever, but she's on a long vacation. Maybe her friend is letting her stay at the beach cottage or city loft for the summer.

22. She or her kid is sick, and needs to be closer to a particular hospital or treatment center.

23. He just needs a shorter commute. He's tired of driving in from the neighboring town.

24. Her last house was flattened by a hurricane or tornado. That's not likely to happen in this part of the country.

25. He used to live there, as a kid, a student, or a young man, and he always regretted moving away.

25 REASONS FOR INITIAL ATTRACTION (BESIDES GOOD LOOKS)

If your character becomes interested in somebody, it's nice if there is a reason besides or in addition to physical attractiveness. Sure, there's nothing wrong with big brown eyes or an athletic physique. Most people like those things! But that's exactly the point: there's nothing special there. It doesn't tell the reader, *Oh my gosh, these two were* made *for each other.*

So here are 25 reasons why your character might sit up straight and take notice of someone. Some of these might work for the beginning of a great friendship as well.

1. In a roomful of vulgar guys, he seems polite and dignified.

2. In a roomful of uptight snobs, she seems like a loveable goofball.

3. He loves the same obscure author, game, or rock band.

4. She makes hilarious jokes.

5. He's the only one who seems to get her jokes.

6. She's shy...and he thinks that's cute.

7. He's gregarious and puts everyone at ease...and that impresses her.

8. They have an experience in common: they both grew up on farms, or they both went to Burning Man.

9. He's impressed by how important her faith is to her.

10. She's impressed by how dedicated to his work he seems to be.

11. His casual comment makes her think about something in a new way.

12. Her voice is sexy.

13. She is pretty clearly a brainiac.

14. He has an amazing sense of personal style.

15. He has an amazing accent.

16. When she smiles, her joy lights up the whole room.

17. He's nice to her pet or her kid.

18. She's animated when she speaks and uses her hands a lot. It's cute.

19. He has an impressive random talent.

20. She stands up for herself.

21. He stands up for a cause she believes in.

22. She seems intense and mysterious.

23. He's in uniform.

24. She smells fantastic.

25. He has the same hopes and dreams as she does...whatever they may be.

4. ACTION

Most of us believe that "actions speak louder than words." No matter what we think or say, what we do says the most about us. The same holds true for the characters in our stories.

Screenwriters, in particular, need to tell their stories through actions as much as words. While some people enjoy introspective, talky films, most audiences want to see things happen.

This section deals with scenes that involve much more action than talk. It also covers ways that people reveal their feelings without stating them directly. Some of these do involve dialogue, but most of them don't. Finally, it lays out different ways that people respond to extreme situations.

500 GREAT WORDS FOR ACTION SCENES

Fistfights and battles, chases and escapes, shootouts and swordplay, flying leaps and crashing cars... Action scenes challenge writers to create compelling choreography, arresting visuals, and visceral character reactions. Here is a thesaurus for writing scenes that will get your readers' hearts pumping. You might even find good inspiration here for the title of your next adrenaline-fueled project. Let's do this!

VERBS

advance	aim	ambush	assault
attack	bail	balance	bang
barrel	bash	batter	battle
beat	bellow	bite	blast
bleed	blind	block	bludgeon
bombard	bounce	brace	breach
break	bullet	burn	burst
bust	butt	careen	catch
challenge	charge	chase	choke
chop	clamp	claw	cleave
climb	cling	clutch	cock
collapse	collide	combust	command
commandeer	corner	cover	cower

crack	crash	crawl	crouch
crumble	crumple	crunch	crush
cuff	cut	dangle	dart
decimate	defeat	defend	defy
deliver	demand	demolish	destroy
dig	dispatch	distract	ditch
dive	divert	dodge	dominate
drag	drift	drip	drive
duck	duel	elbow	electrocute
emerge	evade	exchange	explode
face	fall	falter	fight
fire	flank	flare	flee
fling	flip	fly	follow
force	freeze	gasp	ghost
glare	glide	gouge	grab
grapple	grasp	graze	grimace
grin	grind	grip	growl
grunt	guard	hack	hammer
hang	haul	hijack	hit
hoist	hook	hover	hunt
hurl	hurt	hurtle	ignite

impale	improvise	incinerate	jab
jam	jockey	jump	kick
knee	knock	lacerate	land
lasso	laugh	launch	leap
lift	light up	lob	loom
lurch	maim	maneuver	mangle
mash	mount	obliterate	overcome
overpower	overturn	pant	paralyze
parry	pierce	pivot	plant
plow	plummet	plunge	poke
pounce	pound	propel	protect
pry	pull	pulverize	pummel
pump	punch	puncture	push
race	rage	ram	rear-end
recoil	reel	regain	retrieve
revive	ricochet	rise	roar
roll	ruin	run	rush
sail	save	scoop	scowl
scramble	scrape	scratch	scream
screech	scuttle	sever	shake
shatter	shear	shield	shift

shoot	shout	shove	shred
shudder	singe	skid	skim
slam	slap	slash	slice
slide	sling	slip	smack
smash	smear	snap	snarl
sneak	sneer	somersault	spin
spit	splay	sprawl	sprint
square off	squash	squeal	squeeze
squish	stab	stagger	stalk
stall	stand	startle	steal
stick	sting	stomp	storm
straddle	strain	strangle	stride
strike	struggle	stumble	stun
surround	swagger	sway	sweep
swing	swipe	swoop	take apart
tangle	taunt	tear	tense
thrash	throb	throttle	throw
thrust	thwart	topple	toss
totter	trace	track	trade
trail	transform	trap	tremble
trickle	trip	tumble	twist

unleash	upend	vanquish	vault
veer	whip	whirl	wield
wrap	wrest	wrestle	yank
zigzag	zoom		

accuracy	adrenaline	agility	assailant
assassin	barricade	bastard	blade
blaze	bone	bottle	bravura
brawl	brick	bridge	bruise
bus	chaos	clash	cockpit
concrete	control	damage	danger
daredevil	darkness	destruction	determination
devastation	dust	effort	elevator
enemy	escape	fist	flame
flesh	focus	fracture	fray
fuel	fugitive	fury	gang
getaway	gore	granite	grenade
gut	hazard	headlock	heart
hell	henchman	ice	impact
inferno	instant	invasion	jaw
knuckles	ledge	lightning	madness
marauder	mayhem	menace	mud
oblivion	obstacle	opponent	pain
pavement	pipe	posse	precision
purpose	pursuit	rain	rescue

retreat	ribs	ringleader	roof
scuffle	shadow	shards	shock
sidewalk	siege	skill	skin
skirmish	skull	smoke	socket
soldier	sparks	speed	stance
steam	steel	sternum	stone
strength	survivor	sweat	takedown
target	team	threat	throat
thug	train	tunnel	warrior
water	weight	window	wire
wound	wreckage	wrench	

ADJECTIVES

airborne	audacious	badass	breakneck
breathtaking	brilliant	brutal	catastrophic
decisive	defiant	deranged	desperate
dislocated	disoriented	dizzy	effective
excruciating	exhausted	extreme	fatal
ferocious	fierce	graceful	hard
heedless	insane	lethal	malicious
massive	maximum	messy	mighty

mindless	monstrous	nauseated	nimble
perilous	pitiless	precarious	quick
reckless	relentless	resourceful	ruthless
savage	slick	solid	spectacular
stark	suicidal	surgical	swift
ugly	unconscious	vicious	

500 GREAT WORDS FOR SEX SCENES

A good love scene isn't a sex recess in a story. It furthers the plot in some way, usually by developing the relationship. It also reveals more facets of the characters.

A lot of people feel nervous the first time they write a sex scene. If you focus on the emotions, thoughts, and sensations of the characters, you should be fine. Remember, if you think something is hot, chances are pretty good that other people out there will find it hot, too. Relax, pour a glass of wine if that's right for you, and let the words flow.

VERBS

abandon	ache	arch	arouse
assault	awaken	beg	bite
brace	breathe	brush	buck
burn	bury	capture	caress
choke	circle	claim	clasp
clench	cling	clutch	coax
coil	command	consume	consummate
convulse	course	cover	cradle
crash	crave	crush	cry
cuddle	cup	curl	dart
delve	demand	desire	devour
dip	dive	drag	drink

drive	drown	ease	electrify
enchant	enclose	encourage	enfold
entwine	escalate	explode	explore
exult	fascinate	feast	feed
fill	flare	flex	fling
flood	flush	flutter	force
fuck	fulfill	fuse	galvanize
gasp	gaze	grab	grasp
graze	grip	groan	growl
haul	heave	hiss	hold
immerse	impale	imprison	incite
inflame	inhale	intoxicate	invade
invite	jerk	kiss	kneel
lap	lave	lick	lift
lower	lunge	massage	melt
moan	move	murmur	need
nibble	nip	nuzzle	offer
open	overwhelm	pant	part
penetrate	pet	pinch	play
plunder	plunge	pound	press
provoke	pull	pulse	push

quiver	rack	rage	ram
ravish	redden	relax	relish
restrain	reveal	revel	rise
roam	roar	rock	roll
rub	sate	savor	scoop
scrape	scratch	scream	seek
seep	shake	shatter	shiver
shove	shudder	sigh	sink
skim	skyrocket	slam	slide
slip	snuggle	sob	soothe
spark	spread	squeeze	squirm
stagger	stare	steal	stimulate
stir	strain	stretch	strip
stroke	struggle	stun	succumb
suck	surge	surrender	swallow
sweep	swell	swirl	taste
tease	tempt	thrash	thrill
throb	thrust	tickle	tighten
tilt	tingle	torment	torture
toy	trace	trail	transfix
transport	travel	tremble	trust

tug	tumble	twist	twitch
urge	want	warm	whimper
whisper	wiggle	wind	work
worship	wrap	wriggle	writhe
yank	yearn		

NOUNS

abdomen	act	ankles	ardor
back	beauty	belly	bliss
blood	bond	chest	climax
curves	devastation	ear	ecstasy
edge	elation	embrace	encounter
euphoria	eyes	feet	fever
fingers	flavor	flesh	fragrance
freedom	frenzy	friction	frisson
gentleman	goddess	goosebumps	grace
gratification	greed	hair	hands
heart	hips	hug	hunger
inamorata	instinct	jaw	jolt
joy	legs	lips	lobe
longing	lover	madness	mess

mouth	nails	nape	navel
neck	nerves	obsession	passion
peak	persuasion	plea	pleasure
power	pupils	rake	rapture
rhythm	rumble	rush	satin
satisfaction	scent	scoundrel	seduction
sensation	service	shock	shoulder
siren	skill	skin	soul
soul mate	spice	steel	strength
stubble	sweat	tang	teeth
texture	toes	tongue	torso
touch	treasure	veins	velvet
vision	welcome	wonder	wrists

ADJECTIVES

addictive	alive	alluring	amazed
anguished	bare	blinding	blunt
bold	breathtaking	brilliant	broken
bronzed	brutal	careful	carnal
clever	creamy	dangerous	daring
deep	deft	delicate	delicious

delirious	desperate	determined	devout
drugged	eager	erect	erotic
exposed	exquisite	fast	feral
fervent	fierce	fiery	filthy
firm	forbidden	frantic	full-bodied
furious	generous	gentle	glorious
gorgeous	guttural	hard	heady
heartbreaking	heated	heavy	hesitant
hoarse	hot	hungry	impossible
incandescent	insane	insistent	intense
intimate	irrepressible	irresistible	irrevocable
juicy	languorous	lax	lean
lithe	lovely	luscious	lush
luxurious	magnificent	male	meaningful
merciless	molten	naked	nude
patient	persistent	pliant	plump
potent	primal	pure	radiant
rapid	ravenous	raw	responsive
reverent	rich	rigid	ripe
rosy	rough	savage	scorching
searing	sensual	sexy	shameless

shapely	shy	silken	sincere
sinful	single-minded	slack	slick
slow	smoky	smoldering	smooth
soft	solid	spent	starved
stiff	stormy	strong	sublime
succulent	suggestive	sultry	sumptuous
supple	sweet	swift	tangled
tart	taut	tempestuous	tentative
thick	tousled	unbidden	undone
unguarded	unrelenting	untamed	violent
volatile	voluptuous	vulnerable	wasted
weak	wet	wicked	wild
willing	yielding		

SYNONYMS FOR INTIMATE PARTS OF THE BODY

Some people still believe all romance novels contain hilarious euphemisms for genitalia. Most romance writers don't get too fanciful. Still, sometimes we need synonyms, so I've collected some here. This is really an addendum to the previous list. I thought it would be more helpful to have those separated out.

I personally wouldn't use some of the things on the list, but every writer has her own preferences. Some words may be more appropriate to one point of view than to another, and some might make more sense when your character is just looking at the other person or thinking about sex as opposed to actually having it.

If you are writing a historical story, do the research to make sure you're choosing terms that are appropriate for the period...but remember that many slang terms go way back.

PENIS

This can sometimes be referred to indirectly—"arousal," etc.

cock (probably used the most often in romance)	shaft
arousal	hard-on
phallus	manhood
member	

if he's hard but still has his pants on:

ridge/hard ridge	bulge

SEMEN

seed come vitality

VAGINA

Some of these might benefit from an appropriate adjective in front. Again, this includes ways to refer to the genitalia indirectly.

pussy
(a few people hate this one)
core

slit quim (historical)

sex well

heat wetness

in certain contexts

entrance walls

LABIA

folds petals
female flesh private flesh
secret flesh lips/nether lips

CLITORIS

clit bud bundle of nerves

center of pleasure berry pearl

button most sensitive place

VAGINAL SECRETIONS

juices   cream   honey

nectar   elixir   arousal

Note that almost everybody hates the word moisture. I wouldn't use "secretions," either.

BREASTS

mounds   globes

tits

NIPPLES

peaks   tips   buds

points   beads   nubs

You might want adjectives in front of these: dark tip, tight bud, etc.

BUTTOCKS

ass	butt	backside
derriere	rear	arse (British)
bum (British)	cheeks	globes

50 ACTIONS THAT SHOW ATTRACTION

Let's say the two main characters in a romance, or any story with a romantic subplot, are just starting to get interested in one another. It's way too early for declarations or kisses. How will one of them suspect that the other is into her?

Here are fifty ways, some of them quite subtle, that your characters might demonstrate their feelings—whether they mean to or not.

This list includes indirect cues and obvious signs, and some indicate deeper levels of interest than others. A few of them can also demonstrate feelings of platonic friendship. Remember that for this list, as always, you can substitute genders as you like.

1. He can't stop looking at her.

2. She has trouble meeting his eyes without blushing.

3. He listens intently and leans forward whenever she talks.

4. He inquires about her living situation, or what she likes to do on the weekends... because he's trying to figure out whether she's romantically available.

5. She asks him for a favor—possibly one that involves him coming over to her place, or her coming over to his.

6. She does him an unexpected favor.

7. He asks for his opinion or advice.

8. She reads a book or sees a movie after the woman she likes says it's good.

9. She remembers how he likes his steak, or she gets his coffee shop order right.

10. In a meeting or a classroom, he chooses the seat next to her, even though there are plenty of other empty chairs.

11. She unexpectedly defends him, or his opinion or idea, in a conversation, meeting, or class.

12. He compliments her on something that she cares quite a bit about, but that nobody else ever seems to notice.

13. She wears something frequently or starts wearing her hair a certain way after he says he likes it.

14. He apologizes more than he needs to for a small or nonexistent slight.

15. She gives him a lot of sympathy over small things, like if he has a cold or his weekend plans got ruined.

16. He shows off in front of her or brags about an accomplishment.

17. She stumbles over her words around him, although she is usually articulate.

18. He forgets basic things when he's around her, such as the appointment he needs to get to, or what exactly he came to her store to buy.

19. She fidgets when she's around him or plays nervously with her phone or whatever is close at hand.

20. He notices even slight changes in her expression and body language and asks her what's wrong even when nobody else notices anything is wrong.

21. She talks to him about something that she never discusses with anyone. Her own openness may surprise her.

22. He asks the man he likes an overly personal question...or maybe a few of them.

23. She asks her a lot of questions, just to keep the conversation going.

24. He buys her a gift for her birthday, or just because she said she wanted a particular item...even though they haven't known each other all that long. He might pass it off as no big deal.

25. She plays with her hair when she talks to him.

26. He adjusts his tie when he talks to her.

27. She finds excuses to touch him in casual ways. She might touch his arm to get his attention or to guide him in the right direction if they're walking somewhere together. She might even give him a playful strike on the shoulder in response to something he says.

28. He loans her his jacket because it's cold out.

29. She warns him about bad weather, bad traffic, or a bad-tempered supervisor.

30. He sits or stands up straight when the guy he likes walks into the room.

31. She tilts her head when he's talking and she's listening.

32. He makes a joke for her ears only about the party or the lecture.

33. He laughs more loudly at her joke than she expected.

34. She smiles a whole lot more whenever he's around.

35. His friend makes an excuse to leave them alone together.

36. Her friend says knowingly that she's heard a lot about him.

37. She shows up for a meeting with him several minutes early...even if she makes a habit of being fashionably late.

38. He frantically cleans his apartment before she stops by.

39. She tries to make friends with his daughter, his mom, or his cat.

40. He just happens to turn up at a place where she hangs out or visits regularly.

41. She encourages him to take a bite of her food or a sip of her drink.

42. He offers to drive her or walk her home, even if it's a safe neighborhood and she's only walking a few blocks.

43. She connects with him on social media, and likes his pictures and posts.

44. If her friends talk admiringly about other men—acquaintances, or hot actors—she doesn't join in if he's around.

45. If his friends are joking about gross bodily functions, he doesn't join in if she's around.

46. She makes more racy jokes or sexual innuendoes when she's with him, even if they aren't directed specifically at him.

47. He teases her, but in a flattering way.

48. Her voice becomes ever so slightly softer, gentler, or higher-pitched when she speaks to him.

49. He invites her to a group event, such as a party or a dinner with friends.

50. She gets visibly irritated at someone else flirting with him.

50 ACTIONS THAT SHOW ANIMOSITY

Just as you might want to show a budding friendship or attraction between your characters, you might also need to depict hostility. Your main character might or might not understand what he did to earn this person's dislike or disrespect, but here are fifty ways to demonstrate it. These might also be the actions of people who actually like or love one another, but are fighting and behaving badly.

For these to really show animosity, they have to contrast with how a character treats everyone else. Some of these can be additions to a later list in this book, "25 Ways to Show a Character Is a Jerk," if he acts that way with just about everyone.

Note that some of these actions could be accidental, which might prove useful if you want to sow seeds of misunderstanding between two characters. Some of these are much more hostile than others, although they all fall short of physical violence. You'll want to think about what's appropriate for the level of a conflict, which may increase throughout your story.

In all of these examples, I've used "he" versus "she," just for the sake of clarity. I'm not suggesting that most conflicts are between a man and a woman.

1. He avoids looking her in the eye.

2. She turns her body away from him. It may be a slight or subtle movement.

3. He crosses his arms.

4. She clicks her tongue at something he said.

5. He snorts with disgust at something she said.

6. She rolls her eyes at him.

7. He interrupts her.

8. She exchanges disbelieving looks with others when he talks.

9. He bumps into her or jostles her coffee.

10. She looks at her phone or her watch while he talks.

11. He shakes his head slightly as she talks.

12. She plays the devil's advocate when he expresses an opinion.

13. He thwarts her suggestions even on trivial issues.

14. He speaks to her in a flat tone of voice.

15. He raises his voice when speaking to her.

16. She speaks to him in a tone dripping with sarcasm.

17. He ignores her question or comment.

18. She pretends she doesn't notice that he's walked into the room.

19. He demands to know what she's reading, what she's looking at online, or where she's going, if he thinks it might embarrass her.

20. She insults him, but passes it off as a harmless joke.

21. When she gets good news, he suggests possible down sides.

22. She abruptly stops talking to friends or co-workers when he approaches.

23. He leaves her off of a group invitation to a meeting or a party. He may claim it was an accident.

24. She forgets an appointment with him, or so she says later. Alternately, she cancels it at the last minute for what sounds like a trivial reason.

25. He laughs at something she said when she was being serious.

26. She gives advice and suggestions that imply he's done absolutely everything wrong.

27. He befriends her competitor or rival.

28. She pretends not to notice when he tries to shake hands.

29. He shakes hands using an uncomfortably tight grip.

30. She spreads a false or unflattering story about him.

31. He learns a secret about her that she would rather no one knew—and brings it up.

32. She brings up some small mistake he made months ago.

33. He draws attention to a stain on her blouse, a pimple on her face, or some other flaw.

34. He berates her about an accident or an innocent mistake.

35. He leaves her a mean note.

36. He walks fast, even if she clearly struggles to keep up.

37. When she has trouble carrying something or picking up things she dropped, he doesn't help.

38. She calls him by a nickname he hates.

39. If she's in a position of power, she gives him more than his share of the work, or assigns the worst job to him.

40. He encourages others to join him in making fun of her.

41. She predicts that his job interview, date, or vacation won't go well.

42. He makes fun of something that he knows she likes.

43. She switches off the music he was listening to, or the TV program he was watching.

44. She unfriends or blocks him on social media.

45. He threatens or bullies her via an anonymous account on social media.

46. She damages his property, maybe when no one can see her, or maybe when she can claim it was accidental. She keys his car, spills water on his phone, or runs over his flowerbed.

47. He slams the door, punches a wall, or smashes a plate on the floor.

48. She makes an abrupt retreat: she storms out of the house, abandons camp, or gets off the plane right before departure.

49. She calls him terrible names.

50. He tells her he hopes she dies, or that she should kill herself.

25 RESPONSES TO A CRISIS

When things get really bad, different people react differently. In some cases, their behavior is exactly what one would expect, and in other instances, they reveal new facets of their identities. A person who seems tough may fold like a cheap chair, while a previously unassuming individual may step up to the occasion.

Some of the reactions on this list are reasonable responses to some crises, and inappropriate and counterproductive to others. Some are specific to situations where your characters face a sentient antagonist rather than, say, an illness or a natural disaster.

Your characters' authentic responses to dire events will make your story all the more gripping for a reader. Here are twenty-five possibilities!

1. Physical violence.

2. Freezing up.

   He is completely unable to take action. He may not even be able to move or speak.

3. Bargaining.

   She opens up negotiations with an aggressor, offering something in exchange for a resolution.

4. Persuasion.

   He attempts to appeal to the aggressor's logic or humanity in order to convince her to change course.

5. Seeking comfort.

   She asks someone else for reassuring words, a hand to hold, or a hug.

6. Sarcasm and humor.

   This is his usual strategy for getting through life, and he sticks to it when big problems arise.

7. Crying.

   This may be her main reaction, or something she does before or after taking more productive measures.

8. Blaming.

   Even when it's nobody's fault, he insists that it is.

9. Lashing out.

   While she doesn't actually blame the people around her for what's happening, she does yell at them.

10. Praying.

    She asks God or the deity of her choice to make the crisis go away or keep her company as she goes through it.

11. Fiddling while Rome burns.

    Since everything is terrible, she decides that they may as well have sex or a party.

12. Hiding.

    He cowers in a closet or avoids his friends and acquaintances.

13. Documenting.

    She shoots a video of what's happening or writes about it in her journal in order to make sense of it or serve as a record for others.

14. Analyzing.

    He studies and researches the problem, looking for possible solutions, even when it seems like there aren't any, or there isn't enough time to find them.

15. Nurturing.

    She worries about the impact of the situation on the people around her, and tries to take care of them.

16. Escaping.

He runs away. Depending on the situation, this may prove difficult.

17. Choosing oblivion.

In a different kind of escape, she turns to drugs, alcohol, or even suicide.

18. Taking inventory.

He organizes everything that might prove useful, whether it's canned food, ammo, or a list of friends' phone numbers.

19. Looking for help.

She sets out to find a specialist, a neighbor, or a nearby gunfighter to lend a hand in dealing with the problem.

20. Begging.

He pleads with an aggressor to relent and spare him.

21. Switching sides.

She joins forces with an aggressor in order to survive.

22. Verbal attacks.

He yells at or insults the aggressor.

23. Organizing.

She gets a group to confront the problem together, through a strike, a fundraising push, or an uprising.

24. Deceit.

He attempts to get out of the situation through trickery and distraction.

25. Sacrifice.

She tries to save others in a way that puts herself in danger.

5. DIALOGUE

Dialogue moves the story forward and reveals a lot about the characters. It's also one of the ways that funny stories are funny. Even in a less humorous novel or script, witty or entertaining conversation can make a sweet story less reverent, or provide some much-needed relief to grim or tense proceedings. That's why I began this section with ideas for writing funny dialogue.

All characters have their own way of speaking. Some wouldn't use bad language if they were on fire, while a few may seem almost unable to speak a sentence without a curse word thrown in. The expressions characters use, how much they talk, and when, will probably depend to some extent on their ages and backgrounds, and may also be affected by their gender.

In real life, all of us have expressions and phrases we use frequently. In your story, a character might use the same expression more than once. If someone in your story is meant to be annoying, you could give him an irritating favorite phrase and let him use it frequently.

In some of these lists, I've broken down common parts of conversations. Some of the less usual options might be used ironically by a contemporary character. Although I've included profane expressions, you don't need to make any of your characters talk that way if that's not your style.

I have also included two lists of words and expressions for stories set in medieval England and Victorian England. While nothing can take the place of reading original sources and getting the rhythms of historical speech in your head, they are a good place to start.

25 WAYS TO WRITE FUNNY DIALOGUE

Of course, witty dialogue is all about the execution, but here are some methods that can get you there. One common way to write funny dialogue is by having characters make fun of one another, but this can get old fast. The readers may even get sick of your characters, or think they are a little mean.

When someone in your story says something funny, avoid having other characters overreact to it. If people in the story are slapping their thighs or laughing until they can't breathe at something mildly amusing, the reader may get annoyed. Just remember, a lot of humor grows out of the unique perceptions and points of view of each character.

1. A character is over-dramatic about a situation—or at least, it seems that way to other characters. For instance, he is furious that another player did something shady in his role-playing game, or she is despondent that the jade green dress she ordered is actually emerald green.

2. Someone uses an outlandish or incorrect metaphor, comparing a person, object, or situation to something unexpected.

3. A character is inappropriately candid. (This isn't funny if the character ridicules a vulnerable person.)

4. To a long-winded, convoluted question, someone gives a monosyllabic answer.

5. A character asks someone else a question or a series of questions. The other person doesn't answer, and the character answers her own question(s).

6. Someone misunderstands a question and gives an unrelated answer.

7. A character begins to deliver a clichéd line, but puts an unexpected spin on it.

8. Someone calls another person by a clever nickname.

9. A character pretends to agree with someone, and then adds a sarcastic comment to show she doesn't agree at all.

10. Someone begins to take offense at something another character says about him—and then admits that it's actually true.

11. A character feigns innocence for comic effect. For instance, she acts shocked about the existence of wrongdoing, or pretends to be dismayed that there's no Santa.

12. Someone proclaims his or his friend's superiority in an exaggerated or exceptionally creative fashion.

13. A character anticipates what someone else wants, or is about to say—but she is way off. "I understand. You want me to kill him." "What? No!"

14. Someone tells a lie or makes a claim that nobody would ever believe.

15. A character responds to a surprising proclamation or turn of events in a mild and understated way.

16. Someone makes a casual reference to a bizarre event in her past that nobody knows anything about.

17. A character does an imitation of another character. It's either amusingly bad or hilariously spot on.

18. Someone uses a word or an idiom wrong, or maybe several of them.

19. A character makes a pun or terrible joke, and is very pleased with himself. His being a dork about it is what makes it funny.

20. Someone makes a joke at an inappropriate time, and other characters are unamused.

21. A character says something that, much to her embarrassment, comes out in a suggestive or a self-incriminating way.

22. Someone takes a figure of speech literally, or takes a sarcastic comment in earnest.

23. A character asks someone else a question, but is too distracted to pay attention to or even stick around for the answer.

24. Someone responds to an extremely negative comment or enraged rant in a positive way.

25. A character claims she's said her last word on the subject, and then has to say some more.

WAYS PEOPLE SAY HELLO

Some of these can be combined into one greeting.

"Good morning."

"Morning."

"Hi."

"Hi there!"

"Hiya."

"Hey."

"Hey, dude."

"Hey, man."

"Hey, girl."

"Hey, you."

"Howdy."

"Nice to see you."

"It's been a while."

"Long time no see."

"You're a sight for sore eyes."

"Look what the cat dragged in."

"How are you?"

"How are things?"

"How's it going?"

"How you doing?"

"What's new?"

"What's shaking?"

"Yo, what's up?"

"'Sup?"

"Well, if it isn't (name of person here.)"

"Greetings."

"Good evening."

Additionally, your character could just say the other person's name, with enthusiasm, like this: "David!" "Shoshanna!"

WAYS PEOPLE SAY GOOD-BYE

Again, some of these can be combined.

"Bye."

"Bye now."

"Bye-bye."

"So long."

"See you later."

"Catch you later."

"Catch you on the flip side."

"Later."

"Later, skater."

"I gotta get going."

"I better head out."

"I should be on my way."

"I'm out of here."

"Peace."

"Take it easy."

"Take care."

"It was nice seeing you."

"Nice talking to you."

"Good to see you."

"See you around."

"See ya."

"Ta ta."

"Toodles."

"Ciao."

"Adios."

"Call me!"

"Have a nice day."

"Have a nice night."

"Good night."

WAYS PEOPLE SAY YES

These include answers to factual questions, responses to suggestions, and expressions of agreement.

"Uh-huh."

"Mm-hmm."

"Yup."

"Yeppers."

"Of course."

"Naturally."

"Heck, yes."

"Hell, yeah."

"Affirmative."

"Absolutely."

"Exactly."

"Indeed."

"Correct."

"Precisely."

"Bingo."

"You bet."

"All right."

"Allrighty."

"As far as I know."

"Okay."

"Okey dokey."

"Sounds good."

"I'm down for that."

"I'm game."

"I guess it couldn't hurt."

"Sure thing."

"Sure, why not?"

"I believe so."

"That's right."

"I know, right?"

"That makes sense."

"Damn straight."

"You can say that again."

"Amen to that."

"Preach."

WAYS PEOPLE SAY NO

"I'm not saying no, but…"

"Excuse me?"

"Hold up."

"Nope."

"Nah."

"Naw."

"Uh-uh."

"Nuh-uh."

"Yeah, no."

"How about no."

"Oh God, no."

"Aw, hell, no."

"Yeah, right."

"You wish."

"Get lost."

"Get out of here."

"Give me a break."

"Please."

"Forget it."

"Absolutely not."

"Not hardly."

"Not even close."

"Not a chance."

"Not going to happen."

"No can do."

"No way."

"No way in hell."

"No fucking way."

"Not on your life."

"Not in a million years."

"You've got to be kidding me."

"Are you out of your mind?"

"Seriously?"

"I wish I could."

"I don't think so."

"Let me think about it."

"We'll see."

WAYS PEOPLE VERBALIZE
POSITIVE FEELINGS

"Yesssss."

"Oh, my goodness!"

"Ahhh!"

"Hooray!"

"Woot!"

"Woo hoo!"

"Yee haw!"

"All right!"

"Great!"

"How cool is that?"

"Fabulous!"

"Awesome!"

"Brilliant!"

"Sweet!"

"That's what I'm talking about!"

"Oh yeah!"

"Nice!"

"Yay!"

"Wow!"

"Wooo!"

"Yahoo!"

"Yippee!"

"I love it!"

"Cool!"

"Fantastic!"

"Wonderful!"

"Amazing!"

"Excellent!"

"Hallelujah!"

"Magnificent!"

WAYS PEOPLE VERBALIZE
NEGATIVE FEELINGS

There are so many colorful ways for people to do this, but here are some of the more standard ones. Some of the "Ways People Say No" work here, too.

"Ugh."

"Yikes."

"Ouch."

"Aww, man."

"Drag."

"Jeez."

"Nooo!"

"Oh, shoot."

"Oh, poo."

"Oh, for God's sake."

"For Chrissakes."

"Rats."

"Crap."

"This is bullshit."

"That sucks!"

"Hmmph."

"Wow."

"Grrr."

"Bummer."

"Sheesh."

"Booo."

"Oh, fudge."

"Aw, nuts."

"Oh, for heaven's sake."

"Oh, for fuck's sake."

"Gah!"

"Dang it!"

"This is ridiculous!"

"Unbelieveable."

"Shoot me now."

"Damn it!"

"Damn it all to hell."

"What the fuck?"

"Son of a bitch."

"Alas."

"God damn it."

"What the hell?"

"Shit."

"Fuck this."

WAYS PEOPLE PREFACE
STATEMENTS AND QUESTIONS

Most of the time, you probably want to keep your lines of dialogue somewhat more streamlined than real-life speech. However, extra phrases like this can sometimes reveal the personality or mood of the character. For instance, a more hesitant character might begin more sentences with phrases like, "I could be wrong, but..." or "This could just be me, but..." A phrase before a statement can also add emphasis or irony: "Oh, and by the way, you're fired."

"So get this...."

"Guess what?"

"You know what?"

"You know something?"

"You know..."

"You'll never believe..."

"Listen."

"Look."

"I feel like..."

"I could be wrong, but..."

"Is it just me, or..."

"I'd just like to say..."

"I'll say this much..."

"The way I see it..."

"As far as I'm concerned..."

"From what I understand..."

"If you ask me..."

"Personally, I think..."

"For what it's worth..."

"Just so you know..."

"Just as a heads up..."

"FYI..."

"Not to brag, but..."

"Not for nothing, but..."

"Let me make myself clear."

"Here's the thing."

"The thing is…"

"I've got to tell you…"

"Frankly…"

"Not gonna lie…"

"Believe me…"

"Believe it or not…"

"With all due respect…"

"Don't take this the wrong way, but…"

"I'm sorry, but…"

"Okay, but…"

"At the end of the day…"

"Well…"

"Before I forget."

"Obviously…"

"I gotta be honest here…"

"Actually…"

"Trust me…"

"Believe you me…"

"I swear…"

"No offense, but…"

"Just to play devil's advocate…"

"Forgive me, but…"

"What I want to know is…"

"I mean…"

"By the way…"

"One more thing."

WORDS AND EXPRESSIONS
FROM MEDIEVAL ENGLAND

Almost all of these are straight out of *The Canterbury Tales*, written in the late 1300s, but some are from various versions of King Arthur stories. Some are still in use today, but aren't used nearly as often. I've indicated the meaning or usage wherever I felt that it might not be clear.

Dialogue in a contemporary story set in medieval times is rarely accurate, because it needs to be comprehensible to modern readers. By using a number of archaic words and expressions consistently and avoiding language with too modern a sound, you can achieve a convincing historical feel.

a right good steed

all matter of mirths ("all kinds of fun")

anon ("soon" or "in a little while")

aye

Be he...? ("Is he...?")

be ware ("beware")

begone

betwixt

bid ("ask," "entreat." Past tense: bade.)

bold of his speech

breast (a man's or woman's chest)

bright as any star

by my fay ("by my faith")

by my troth ("I swear")

by your leave

certes ("assuredly")

chérie (endearment, to a woman: "dear," "darling")

choleric ("bad-tempered")

churlish

cursed be that day

dalliance (brief sexual
relationship)

demoiselle ("damsel" is an
abbreviated version of this.
It means "lady," and may
be used in direct address)

ere/ere long
("before"/"before long")

fair ("attractive," of a woman;
also used in place of "nearly")

fie on thee (used the
same way as, "screw you,"
"the hell with you")

for Christ's love (used the
same way as, "for God's sake")

fresh as a rose

God defend you/God
save you (other ways of
saying "God bless you")

God you speed

grammercy ("thank you")

haply ("perhaps")

have some drop of pity

come hither

dally

deem ("consider," "judge")

dumb as a tree ("silent")

fain ("pleased," "willing")

fellow (also "good
fellow"; used to address
a common man)

fierce as any lion

for the nonce ("for
the time being")

full (used to mean "very,"
as in "full wise")

God's teeth (a curse)

gone to ground like a fox
("went into hiding")

grievous (often used to
describe news, or a wound)

hark ("listen")

he acquitted himself
well ("he did well")

Ho!/Ho there!
("Hey!"/"Hey you!")

hold you still ("hold still")

hold your peace ("be quiet")

I cannot say ("I don't know")

I cry you mercy ("I
beg your pardon")

I marvel that... ("I'm
surprised that...")

I pray you of your courtesy
(the same as, "if you
would be so kind")

I say not so ("that's not
what I'm saying")

imprimis ("first of all")

in no wise ("in no way")

in sooth ("to tell the truth")

in this wise ("in this way")

Jesú/Jesú Christus
("Jesus"/"Jesus Christ")

jolly as a pie (meaning
"jolly as a magpie")

knave (a boy or servant; may
also mean a scoundrel)

leech ("doctor")

leman (female lover
or sweetheart)

list ("want," "like")

low company ("bad company")

lusty ("healthy," "robust")

mark me well ("listen to me")

may the Virgin keep thee safe

merde (a vulgar curse)

meseems ("it seems to me")

messires

milady

milord

mine (often used instead
of "my" before a noun)

mischance

most like ("most likely")

must needs ("need(s) to")

naked as a needle

natheless ("nonetheless")

naught

Bryn Donovan

nay

nigh ("near"; "nearly")

of a surety ("definitely")

overlong ("too long")

perilous

pray ("please")

privily ("secretly" or "confidentially")

red as any fox

sennight ("week")

sirrah (used to address a man or boy of lower rank; an insult)

slut (a woman who doesn't keep herself clean)

succor

tarry

thou ("you," as the subject of a verb)

treacherous

never was there such another (storm, knight, etc.)

no more will I ("neither will I")

on the morrow

passing ("very")

prate (a disparaging way to say "talk")

prithee (an abbreviation of "pray thee;" also means "please")

queint ("vagina")

sanguine ("cheerful"; can also refer to a ruddy complexion)

simpleton

slay

stalwart

swain (a young male lover)

thee ("you," as an object of a verb or preposition)

thy ("your")

trow ("think," "believe")

trull ("prostitute")

varlet (a servant, particularly a knight's page; by mid-1500s, it meant a dishonest man)

touching him ("concerning him")

wax ("grow," "become," as in "it waxes late")

What cheer?/What cheer do you have? ("How are you?")

What ho? ("What's this?")

What wilt thou say?

whether he will or no ("whether he wants to or not," "whether he wants it or not")

whilst

whosoever

will he or nill he (same as "whether he will or no")

with full glad heart

witless ("foolish")

woe

yea

yellow as wax

yeoman (a landowner of a class beneath the gentry; may be used in direct address)

yonder

your wont ("your desire," or "your tendency")

WORDS AND EXPRESSIONS FROM VICTORIAN ENGLAND

Most of these words and phrases are used today, but far less frequently. To create this list, I worked from the dialogue in the novels of Charlotte and Emily Brontë, Charles Dickens, Anthony Trollope, and Sir Arthur Conan Doyle, as well as *Passing English of the Victorian Era*, published in 1909. I haven't included much street slang or any Cockney rhyming slang, delightful as it is, because their application is so specific and because so many excellent resources for them exist online.

Characters in British Victorian novels use more adverbs than in contemporary ones, particularly in negative contexts: "a beastly country," "cruelly unjust," "dreadfully poor," and so on. Even if you are accustomed to eschewing adverbs in your writing, you may want to make some use of them in historical conversations.

Reading a few Victorian novels will give you an ear for the dialogue. Sentence constructions, in particular, are different and more elaborate in Victorian conversations than in present-day speech.

a good deal/a great deal ("a lot")

a small matter/no matter ("no big deal")

abominable

agreeable (may describe not only a person but also a situation)

amiable

at your peril ("at your own risk")

away (lower class usage: a euphemism for "in prison")

Bah! (an expression of disgust)

bang up to the elephant ("perfect" – this later got shortened to "bang up," as in "doing a bang-up job")

barmy ("crazy," "mad")

beast (used as an insult)

before you can say Jack Robinson ("in no time")

between the Devil and the deep blue sea (similar to "between a rock and a hard place")

blackguard

bless my soul

bootlicker ("sycophant")

butter upon bacon ("more than enough")

by George

by Jove

by-the-bye ("by the way")

capital ("excellent," as in "a capital idea")

chafed (annoyed: "you are a little chafed")

charming

clever

Cock of the Walk (a leader, or a confident, domineering man)

coming a cropper (failing, or having a stroke of very bad luck)

confound it/confound you ("damn it"/"damn you")

contrivance (may mean an invention or a scheme)

cordial

costermonger (someone who sells fruits and vegetables, usually from a cart on the street)

countenance

creature (used of people: "dear creature," "poor creature," "be a reasonable creature")

cross (as in "grumpy")

cruel (frequently used in the same way contemporary North Americans use "mean")

dash it all (a more polite version of "damn it all")

dear me

delightful

detestable

devilish (used to modify an adjective, such as "devilish good-natured")

disgraceful

distressing

diverting

double-dealing ("backstabbing," "treacherous")

doubtless

dreadful

drunk as a lord (a middle and lower class expression)

dull as ditchwater (this is the original expression, possibly coined by Dickens, which later changed to "dull as dishwater")

everything is nice in your garden (a mildly reproachful response to a boast)

extraordinary

falsehood

feeling low (a common way to say "sad"; also, "low in spirits")

fellows (frequently, the way a man refers to other men)

a fine fellow

in fine fettle (in good shape, or well organized)

fond

folly

fool/foolish

foolish fancy (a silly idea or notion)

for shame (used as a reproach)

frightful/frightfully

ghastly

glad to hear of it ("I am glad to hear of it;" "I hope he will be glad to hear of it")

gloomy

good God

good gracious/good gracious me

good-humored

grand ("Isn't that a grand idea?")

grieved (not only used in reference to death: bad news or bad luck may leave someone "grieved")

grouse ("grumble")

hang it all (used in the same way as "damn it," to express frustration)

hard (used in the same way as "mean," as in, "you say such hard things")

hard as nails

haste ("make haste" means "hurry," and "hasty" means "quick")

he worships the golden calf ("he only cares about profit")

heaven and earth (used in the same way as, "for heaven's sake")

hindrance

hoodwinked

horrid

hungry as a hunter

I assure you ("most assuredly," "most assuredly not," and "most assuredly so" are also commonly used)

I can't give over ("I can't let it go")

I dare say

I entreat you

I give you my sacred honour that ("I promise you that")

I say... (a common beginning of a sentence)

I wonder that... ("I'm surprised that...")

idleness

if I may inquire

if you please

I'll be bound ("I bet")

I'm sure (sometimes used at the end of sentences: "I don't know, I'm sure." "I'm certain" is used in the same way.)

ill-bred

impertinence

in a twinkling ("in a moment")

insolence

Indeed? ("Really?")

it is just the thing ("it is popular"; "it is commonly done")

jolly

let me bear you company ("let me keep you company")

loathsome

Love bless you/Lord love you

lucky dog (a lucky man)

madness (like "lunacy," often used to describe plans and situations)

mamma (used by many children and adult women to address and refer to their mothers)

mean (used as a synonym of "stingy")

minx (mischievous girl or young woman)

monstrous

my blood is up ("I'm upset")

my dear boy/fellow/girl/sir/lady/child

my good sir/my worthy sir

naughty

no use flogging a willing horse

nor did I ("neither did I")

not a matter of much consequence

not to be endured

oh, dear/oh, dear me

oh, my stars

odious

on the square ("honest")

palaver (idle or pointless discussion)

paltry

papa (used by many children and adult women to address and refer to their fathers)

peevish

perfect lady (used satirically on the streets, to describe someone who's anything but)

pitiful

pleasant ("a pleasant journey," "a pleasant evening")

Pooh! Pooh! (a dismissive expression)

portionless (without a regular allowance)

provoking ("irritating")

Pshaw! (an expression of disparagement)

quarrelsome

queer ("strange")

quite right ("absolutely"; "quite correct" is also used often)

scarcely

sick at heart ("very upset")

speak plainly

spruce (neat or stylish)

stupified

that won't answer ("that won't work")

throw him over ("abandon him")

scoundrel

scuttler (a tough young person of the streets)

silent as the tomb

splendid

suitable

sulky

that is nothing to the purpose ("that doesn't matter")

thrashed ("beaten")

to be sure

trifle

Tut, tut! (an expression of admonishment)

uncivil

uncommonly

unfeeling

ungenerous

unjust

unmanly

unwell

up to the scratch ("sufficient," "good enough")

upon my life

upon my word

vainglorious

vexed

victuals (food; provisions)

vulgar (often used the same way as "tacky" or "trashy," to describe both things and people)

was desirous of ("wanted")

well-bred

What can you mean?/Whatever can you mean? ("What do you mean?")

What next? (a common response to an unbelievable statement)

What the deuce...? ("What the heck...?")

What the devil...? ("What the devil do you mean?" "What the devil's the use?")

woeful

wickedness

with all my heart

Would you be good enough to...? (used when asking a favour; also, "Could you have the goodness to...?")

wretched

you are very good/you are very kind

you do me honour

your obedient servant (a popular closing for a letter; also, "your humble servant")

6. CHARACTER NAMES

Some of us take forever to figure out what to call the people in our stories—and with good reason. Often, one of the first things our reader learns about a character is his or her name. For a novel, the names of the main characters are right there in the blurb or on the back cover.

If the names sound too fake, that can turn people off, although there is a lot of leeway in speculative genres such as science fiction, fantasy, and paranormal romance. When the character names of a historical story are too modern, readers will roll their eyes. Bad character names can even keep people from buying a book in the first place.

Getting the right names for characters is a passion of mine, and I'm going to share a few suggestions to make your choices reader-friendly. It's only my opinion, so see what works for you.

1. Whenever possible, choose names that most readers will be able to pronounce in their heads, at least for your main characters. Granted, this may be a challenge for some time periods and places.

2. If you pick an unusual first name, you might want to go with a normal surname ("Indiana Jones" is a great example.) Conversely, if you have a common first name, you might want a more evocative last name to give your character some flair ("Mary Poppins," for instance.) Then again, you might want the character to sound like a very average person...even if it turns out she's anything but.

3. Avoid writing a conversation where the character explains why she is named what she is ("Actually, my full name is Andromeda. My mother is an astronomer, you see...") It's overdone. If the name is so weird that it absolutely requires explaining, pick a more believable one.

4. If you are writing a fantasy or science fiction story, the characters from the same culture should have a similar logic to their names. For instance, don't name one elf Silverleaf and another elf Bob.

5. Make sure all of your characters don't have names that start with the same letter, or else your reader will have a terrible time keeping them straight. Giving siblings names that start with the same letter is fine, because it reminds the reader that they are related.

6. Avoid having the same number of syllables in everyone's first and last names. Mix it up a little.

7. Use nicknames to convey relationships. For instance, the first time one of your character shortens the name of another one—calling her "Ro" instead of "Rosemary," for instance—it can be an exciting signal to the reader that they've become closer. Family members and old friends may have childhood nicknames for your character that nobody else uses in her adult life. In some communities, everyone may go by nicknames.

Okay, enough advice. On to the lists!

NAMES FROM VIKING-ERA SCANDINAVIA

I found most of the names on this list in Norse sagas that describe the Viking age in the 900s and early 1000s. I also looked at historical documents dating from around that time.

This list includes Anglicized names, and I have excluded many names that I felt would befuddle most English-speaking readers. Some of these names may still be difficult, or sound odd—in fact, one of the men's names is literally Odd—but they will give your Viking historical novel or romance an authentic feel.

I've also listed last names that people earned, such as Sweyn Forkbeard and Erik the Red. You could have a lot of fun making up surnames like this for your characters. Some of the ones here seem kind of mean, but if you've ever read any of the sagas, this will not surprise you.

WOMEN

Agata	Ádisa	Alfifa	Arnfasta
Arnóra	Ása	Asgerd	Aslaug
Asny	Astrid	Astrior	Asvor
Atla	Aud	Bera	Bergthóra
Bersa	Birna	Borga	Brynhild
Dagmar	Dalla	Droplaug	Edda
Elfdisa	Eyfura	Folka	Freydis
Frigg	Geirrid	Gerd	Grima
Grimhild	Gróa	Gudrid	Gudrun
Gudny	Gunnhildr	Hadda	Haldora

Halla	Hallbera	Hallgerda	Hallkatla
Helga	Herbord	Herdís	Hilda
Holmkel	Hungerd	Ingibiorg	Idun
Jódís	Jofrid	Jórunn	Katla
Kol	Kolfrosta	Kolga	Kristrún
Luta	Nál	Nauma	Olof
Osk	Randalin	Ragnhild	Rannveig
Ríkví	Sága	Saldís	Sif
Signy	Sigrid	Skaga	Svala
Svanhild	Steingerd	Swala	Thora
Thorbera	Thorbjörg	Thordis	Thorgerd
Thurid	Ulfrún	Unna	Valka
Vigdis			

MEN

Alfarin	Asmund	Asolf	Atli
Audolf	Bard	Bearne	Bergfinn
Björn	Bodvar	Bolli	Bork
Bran	Brand	Dofri	Egil
Einar	Eldearn	Erik	Eyjolf
Eywind	Finnbogi	Gestr	Gisli

Glum	Grettir	Grimr	Grímur
Gunnar	Gunnbjorn	Gunnlaug	Hafgrim
Haldor	Hagbard	Harald	Heimir
Helgi	Hermund	Illugi	Ingimundur
Ivar	Jofrid	Jokul	Jorund
Ketil	Leif	Odd	Ofeig
Olaf	Olvir	Ogmund	Önundur
Ondott	Orund	Ossur	Raknar
Randwer	Raven	Rerir	Rolf
Sigi	Sigurd	Skuli	Snorri
Solvi	Soti	Steinolf	Stymir
Sweyn	Thrand	Thoralf	Thorarin
Thorfinn	Thorgrim	Thorgunna	Thorir
Thorkel	Thorsteinn	Thorvald	Thrond
Ufeig	Uspak	Vali	Vestein
Vestmar	Viglund	Wolf	

SURNAMES – WOMEN

Ásbrandsdóttir	Bárðsdóttir	Baugsdóttir
Bjarnardóttir	Bolladóttir	Brynjólfsdóttir
Egilsdóttir	Einarsdóttir	Flosadóttir

Gamlisdóttir	Gilsdóttir	Grímsdóttir
Hallkelsdóttir	Hermundardóttir	Höskuldursdóttir
Hrútssdóttir	Ingjaldsdóttir	Jónsdóttir
Kollsdóttir	Konalsdóttir	Ófeigsdóttir
Oddsdóttir	Olofsdótter	Onundardóttir
Ósvífrsdóttir	Sigurðsdóttir	Skaftadóttir
Snorradóttir	Steinsdóttir	Sturludóttir
Tindsdóttir	Valbrandsdóttir	Vestarsdóttir
Yngvarsdóttir	Sunbeam	Witchface
the Fair	the Deep-Minded	the Haughty
the High-Counseled	the Low	the Slender

SURNAMES – MEN

Asbrandson	Ásvaldsson	Bollason
Bolverkson	Egilson	Eriksson
Estridsson	Geitirsson	Gormsson
Gnupasson	Gudlaugsson	Hafgrimson
Hámundarson	Haraldsson	Harðbeinsson
Herjolfsson	Hoskuldsson	Hrólfsson
Ingjaldsson	Ketilsson	Kollsson
Leifsson	Magnusson	Marson

Ólafsson	Önundarson	Skallagrímsson
Súrsson	Tryggvason	Bloodaxe
Clubfoot	Combhood	Dry-Frost
Flatnose	Gatebeard	Halt-Foot
Greycloak	Most-Beard	Ironpate
Longchin	Rough-Foot	Treefoot
Wall-Eye	Wooden-Leg	the Black
the Bounteous	the Broad	the Burner
the Crow	the Fox	the Greyhaired
the Learned	the Masterful	the Peacock
the Sage	the Smiter	the Strong
the Unwashed	the Victorious	the Proud
the Thick	the Wealthy	the Wise
the Worm-Tongue		

NAMES FROM MEDIEVAL ENGLAND

This list might also be helpful if you're writing a high fantasy with swords and sorcery. Naming trends didn't change nearly so quickly in past centuries as they do now, so it's a good resource for your English Renaissance or Tudor-era story as well.

My sources include battle histories, subsidy rolls, and *A Dictionary of English Surnames*. I also included just a few names from the King Arthur legends.

MEN

Adam	Adelard	Aglovale	Alan
Aland	Albert	Aldred	Alexander
Alfred	Alisander	Alphonse	Amis
Anselm	Arnold	Arthur	Balin
Bardolph	Barnabas	Bartholomew	Basil
Baudwin	Bennet	Berenger	Bernard
Bertram	Blaise	Bliant	Brom
Bryce	Castor	Cederic	Cerdic
Charles	Cyr	Daniel	David
Denis	Diggory	Dinadan	Drogo
Edgar	Edward	Edwin	Egbert
Elias	Eliot	Eluard	Emory
Eustace	Everard	Faramond	Frederick

Fulke	Gabriel	Galleron	Gamel
Gareth	Geoffrey	George	Gerald
Gerard	Gervase	Gilbert	Giles
Godwin	Gregory	Griffith	Gunter
Guy	Hamon	Hamond	Hardwin
Hector	Henry	Herbert	Herman
Hildebrand	Hubert	Hugh	Humphrey
Ingram	Isaac	Isembard	Ives
James	Jasper	Jeremy	Jocelyn
Jordan	Joseph	Lambert	Laurence
Leland	Leofwin	Lionel	Lucan
Lucius	Mabon	Manfred	Mark
Martin	Matthew	Maynard	Merek
Michael	Miles	Milo	Nicholas
Nigel	Noah	Ogier	Osric
Paul	Percival	Peter	Philip
Piers	Randel	Ranulf	Reginald
Richard	Robert	Roger	Roland
Rolf	Rowan	Sampson	Sayer
Silas	Solomon	Theobald	Thomas
Thurstan	Timm	Tobias	Tristram

Turstin	Ulric	Urian	Walter
Warin	Warner	William	Wolfstan
Wymond			

WOMEN

Acelina	Adelina	Aelina	Agnes
Aldith	Alice	Alma	Althea
Alyson	Amelina	Amicia	Anais
Anne	Artemisia	Athelina	Audry
Augusta	Avina	Barbetta	Beatrice
Berta	Blanche	Brangwine	Bridget
Caesaria	Cassandra	Catelin	Caterina
Cecily	Celestria	Christina	Clare
Constance	Dameta	Delia	Dionisia
Douglas	Edeva	Edith	Eglenti
Elaine	Eleanor	Elizabeth	Elle
Elysande	Emeline	Emma	Etheldreda
Eva	Evaine	Evelune	Felicia
Florence	Floria	Genevieve	Gisela
Giselle	Gracia	Gratia	Guinevere
Gundred	Gwendolen	Helewisa	Ida

Ingerith	Isabeau	Isemay	Isolda
Ivette	Joan	Johanna	Joya
Joyce	Juliana	Justina	Laudine
Lavina	Legarda	Lena	Letia
Leticia	Lia	Lillian	Linota
Lovota	Lucia	Lunete	Magdalen
Margaret	Margery	Marie	Marion
Martha	Mary	Mathilde	Maud
Milisant	Mirielda	Molly	Muriel
Nesta	Nicola	Odelina	Oliva
Orella	Oswalda	Paulina	Petronilla
Regina	Richolda	Roana	Rosa
Rosamund	Roxanne	Sabina	Sapphira
Sarah	Sela	Sigga	Sophronia
Susanna	Swanhild	Sybil	Tephania
Theda	Thora	Venetia	Viviane
Ysmeine			

SURNAMES

This list includes patronyms, occupational names, and place names. You will need to research whichever last name you choose to make sure that it makes sense for your character.

Achard	Alder	Arundel	Ashdown
Atwood	Auber	Bainard	Baker
Ballard	Barnes	Basset	Bauldry
Baxter	Beaumont	Becker	Bellecote
Beringar	Bertran	Bigge	Bolam
Bosc	Bouchard	Brewer	Brickenden
Brooker	Brooker	Browne	Burrel
Burroughs	Butler	Cambray	Campion
Campion	Canouville	Capron	Capron
Cardon	Cardonell	Carpenter	Carter
Cecil	Challener	Challenge	Chauncy
Chauncy	Cherbourg	Clarke	Clay
Colleville	Comyn	Cooke	Cooper
Corbet	Corbin	Courcy	Court
Cross	Crump	Cumin	Custer
d'Albert	d'Ambray	Dale	Danneville
Darcy	Dean	de Balon	de Beauvais
de Bethencourt	de Bethencourt	de Blays	de Challon

de Civille	de Coucy	de Erley	de Ferrers
de Grandmesnil	de Grey	de Ireby	de Lacy
de la Haye	de la Pole	de la Porte	de la Reue
de la Roche	de Logris	de Lorris	de Maris
de Montfort	Deschamps	de Servian	des Roches
Destain	Dodd	Drake	Draper
Dumont	Durandal	Durville	Duval
Duval	Dyer	Emory	Evelyn
Faintree	Faucon	FitzAlan	FitzOsbern
Fitzroy	Fletcher	Ford	Foreman
Forester	Fox	Fuller	Gael
Gary	Gaveston	Giffard	Gillian
Gilpin	Glanville	Godart	Godefroy
Graves	Griffen	Grosseteste	Guideville
Gurney	Hachet	Harcourt	Hauville
Hawthorn	Hayward	Hendry	Holland
Holmes	Hood	Hope	Hughes
Ide	la Mare	Lamb	Langdon
Latham	Lea	le Blanc	le Blanc
le Conte	le Grant	le Grant	le Orphelin

le Roux	le Savage	Lister	Lucy
Lynom	Malet	Mallory	Mallory
Manners	Marchmain	Marshal	Martel
Mason	Mathan	Mathan	May
Medley	Mercer	Mortimer	Mortmain
Mowbray	Napier	Nash	Nesdin
Neuville	Noyers	of Benwick	of Cleremont
of Warwick	of Wichelsea	Osmont	Papon
Parmenter	Parry	Parry	Paschal
Patris	Payne	Perci	Perroy
Peveril	Picard	Port	Prestcote
Rainecourt	Raleigh	Rames	Renold
Reviers	Roger	Rolfe	Rowntree
Saint-Clair	Saint-Germain	Saint-Leger	Sawyer
Seller	Shepherd	Slater	Taylor
Teller	Thibault	Thorne	Tilly
Tull	Vaughan	Vaux	Verdun
Vernon	Ward	Watteau	Weaver
Webber	Wells	Wilde	Willoughby
Wood	Wright	Writingham	

NAMES FROM REGENCY ENGLAND

The Regency period is exceptionally popular in historical romance. This list is a good reference for any project set in England from the Georgian through the Victorian era.

The Regency period lasted from 1811 to 1820. To create this list, I used various parish records from that period. I also looked at portions of UK Census Returns of 1801 and 1821, and parts of Burke's Peerage 1826. Although these latter sources were not dated exactly to the Regency period, they were close enough to contribute to an accurate list.

Many of these names would have had nicknames, such as "Nora" for "Honora" and "Molly" for "Mary." I've only listed diminutives if they were given names in their own right. Some of the first names here are unusual for the time. Although I haven't done a quantified study, an asterisk indicates a name that showed up often in the records I consulted.

I didn't do a surname list here because it overlapped so much with the surnames in the medieval list, as well as the list of the most popular U.S. surnames at the end of this section.

WOMEN

Abigail	Agnes	Albina	Alice*
Alicia	Amelia	Amy	Angel
Ann*	Anne*	Arabella	Augusta
Awellah	Barbara	Beatrice	Betsey
Betty*	Bridget	Caroline	Catherine*
Cecilia	Charity	Charlotte*	Christianna
Deborah	Diana	Dinah	Dorothea
Dorothy	Edith	Eleanor*	Eliza*

Elizabeth*	Ellen*	Emily	Emma
Emmeline	Esther*	Fanny*	Florentia
Frances*	Frederica	Georgiana	Georgina
Grace*	Hannah*	Harriet*	Helen
Helena	Henrietta	Hester	Honora
Horatia	Isabel*	Isabella	Jane*
Jean	Jemima	Jenny	Jessie
Joan	Joanna	Joyce	Judith
Julia	Juliana	Juliet	Katherine
Kitty	Laura	Lavinia	Leah
Letitia	Lilias	Louisa	Lucy*
Lucy-Anne	Lydia	Madalene	Margaret
Maria*	Marianne	Marina	Margaret*
Marjorie	Martha*	Mary*	Mary Ann*
Matilda	Miriam	Modesty	Nancy*
Patience	Peace	Peggy	Phillis
Phyllis	Phoebe	Priscilla	Prudence
Rachel*	Rebecca*	Rose	Ruth
Sally*	Sarah*	Selina	Sophia*
Susan*	Susannah	Tabitha	Teresa
Theodosia	Unity		

MEN

Aaron	Abraham*	Adam	Adolphus
Albinus	Albion	Alexander*	Algernon
Allan	Ambrose	Americus	Andrew
Anthony	Archibald	Arthur	Augustus
Aylmer	Baldwin	Barnard	Benedict
Benjamin*	Brook	Carew	Cecil
Charles*	Christmas	Christopher*	Coape
Colin	Cornelius	Daniel*	David*
Donald	Dudley	Duncan	Edmund*
Edward*	Edwin	Eli	Elias
Emanuel	Ephraim	Erasmus	Ernest
Evan	Ewan	Ezra	Felton
Francis*	Frederick	George*	Gerard
Gibbs	Giles	Gilbert	Graham
Guy	Harcourt	Harry	Henry*
Herbert	Honor	Horace	Hudson
Hugh*	Isaac*	Jacob	Jahleel
James*	Jasper	Jeffrey	Jeremy
Jerome	John*	Jonathan*	Joseph*
Joshua	Josiah	Josias	Kenneth

Laurence	Leonard	Levi	Lewis
Lodge	Loftus	Ludlow	Luke
Mark	Martin	Matthew*	Meshach
Michael	Miles	Morgan	Moses
Nash	Nathaniel	Neil	Nicholas
Noah	Norman	Obadiah	Oliver
Owen	Patrick	Percy	Percival
Peregrine	Peter*	Philip*	Phineas
Ralph	Reginald	Reuben	Richard*
Robert*	Roger	Rollo	Sampson
Samuel*	Seth	Shadrack	Sherborne
Silas	Simon	Solomon	Stephen
Theophile	Thomas*	Timothy	Walter
William*			

200 NAMES FROM THE WILD WEST

The list of Regency names will actually give you plenty of good ideas for naming characters in an American Western, and you'll be able to tell which ones are too high-faluting to import into your Wild West town (although even those might be good for one of your city slicker characters.) Here are some first names of real people in the 19th-century Western United States. They are outlaws, lawmen, buffalo soldiers, rodeo performers, soldiers who fought at the Alamo, railroad laborers, gold prospectors, prostitutes, business owners, entertainers, and more.

Several names on the list are unusual, and some sound like nicknames. They may still be given names, or in some cases, a person's nickname may have become so common that his Christian name was forgotten, even for official documents.

Many of these names are English or German in origin, and some of them seem to be American inventions. Names with an asterisk belonged to Mexicans or Mexican Americans. Two asterisks indicate a Chinese name, spelled as it was on the census records. There were far fewer Chinese women than Chinese men in the Wild West, and I was unable to find any on census records, so I don't have any listed here.

This list does not include names of Native Americans, as far as I know, because I don't want to contribute to any errors. You'll need to look into a Native American character's particular background and history and consider factors of cultural assimilation in order to find an appropriate name.

WOMEN

Adaline	Aleda	Almira	Alpha
America	Antonia*	Artemicia	Aurora
Banica	Barbary	Belle	Beulah
Birdie	Blanche	Caldonia	Calsey

Candelaria*	Chastelle	Clementine	Comfort
Cordelia	Cory	Della	Dina
Dixie	Dolly	Donita	Drusilla
Edgarda	Effie	Elisa	Ernestine
Elnora	Etta	Eugenia	Eunice
Faustina	Faye	Freda	Fredricka
Guadelupe*	Gussie	Helentha	Helvina
Hepsibah	Iola	Isadora	Iva
Kittie	Jewell	Jovenita*	Lena
Lissie	Lola	Lotta	Lovina
Luella	Lulu	Malena	Malinda
Marietta	Mattie	Medina	Minerva
Missouri	Myra	Nannie	Narcissa
Nellie	Nesta	Nettie	Nicolasa*
Parthenia	Patsie	Pearl	Philena
Pleasant	Reta	Reva	Rosalia
Rosetta	Sadie	Salina	Sallie Jane
Sirena	Solana	Sura	Temperance
Thresia	Trinidad*	Una	Ursula
Versie Mae	Victoriana*	Vina	Wilhelmina
Zerelda	Zola		

MEN

Adison	Alladin	Alvis	Antone
Axel	Bass	Bing	Boone
Bose	Bruno	Burrell	Buster
Camillus	Chambers	Chancy	Clinton
Cornelius	Dallas	Delton	Dewitt
Elfego*	Ellwood	Emil	Emmett
Ervine	Eulogio*	Fidelous	Fine
Fletcher	Floyd	Gregorio*	Grover
Gustavus	Ham	Hamilton	Hampton
Herman	Hilliard	Hiram	Holden
Hugo	Isham	Jin**	Judd
Lacon	Lafayette	Lamoyne	Larken
Launcelot	Leander	Leonidas	Lester
Levi	Lewellyn	Lin**	Lot
Loyal	Lucius	Lyman	Mack
Major	Marlin	Marquess	Maximino*
Melchior	Merritt	Millard	Milo
Monroe	Montford	Mose	Newton
Orlindo	Paden	Pious	Pliney
Preston	Prince	Prudencio*	Pryor

Quan**	Quincy	Ransom	Roscoe
Shelby	Simeon	Socorro*	Squire
Stillman	Temple	Tiburcio*	Tuck
Uriah	Ventura*	Volney	Warner
Washington	Wiley	Worth	Wright

NAMES FROM WORLD WAR II-ERA U.S. AND GREAT BRITIAN

If you need names for soldiers, pilots, nurses, Rosie the Riveters and Land Girls, look no further. This list can also be useful for any project set in the U.S. or the U.K. from the 1930s through the 1950s. You might even find the perfect name for an older character in your contemporary novel. Many of the names on this list are still popular today.

For the most part, names were pretty similar on both sides of the pond. The names marked with an asterisk, however, seem to be more typical in the U.K. than in the U.S. in this period.

WOMEN

Agnes	Alice	Alma	Anna
Annie	Barbara	Beatrice	Bernice
Bertha	Betty	Catherine	Clara
Dolores	Doris	Dorothy	Edith
Edna	Elaine	Eleanor	Elizabeth
Ella	Elsie	Emma	Esther
Ethel	Evelyn	Florence	Frances
Geraldine	Gertrude	Gladys	Gloria
Hazel	Helen	Irene	Jane
Jean	Josephine	Juanita	June
Leona	Lillian	Lois	Lorraine

Louise	Lucille	Mabel	Marie
Marion	Marjorie	Margaret	Martha
Mary	Maud*	Mildred	Minnie
Myrtle	Nancy	Norma	Opal
Patricia	Pearl	Phyllis	Rita
Rose	Ruby	Ruth	Sarah
Shirley	Thelma	Vera	Virginia
Wanda	Wilma	Yvonne*	

MEN

Albert	Alvin	Anthony	Archibald*
Arthur	Benjamin	Bernard	Carl
Charles	Chester	Clarence	Clyde
Cyril*	Dale	Daniel	David
Donald	Douglas	Edgar	Edward
Edwin	Ernest	Eugene	Everett
Francis	Frank	Fred	Frederick
Geoffrey*	George	Gilbert	Glenn
Harold	Harry	Harvey	Henry
Herbert	Howard	Hugh*	Ian*
Jack	James	John	Joseph

Kenneth	Lawrence	Leo	Leonard
Louis	Marvin	Maurice	Milton
Nigel*	Oscar	Paul	Percy*
Peter	Ralph	Raymond	Richard
Robert	Roy	Russell	Samuel
Sidney*	Stanley	Thomas	Vernon
Victor	Virgil	Walter	Warren
Wayne	Willard	William	

200 NAMES FOR CONTEMPORARY HEROINES

When you're naming characters for a novel or script set in the present day, you can turn to a baby name book or website. However, that means wading through thousands of choices, many of them difficult to pronounce or hard to imagine using for an adult in a contemporary setting. This is my attempt to make it a little bit easier.

Many names on this list are popular for women in their 20s, 30s, and 40s in the United States. I have avoided some choices with negative connotations or baggage (although any one of them might carry baggage for you). I've curated some rarer names as well. I hope you can find the right moniker here for your quirky, brave, gorgeous, brainy, compassionate, and/or hilarious heroine!

1. Abigail

2. Aisha

3. Alexandra/Alexandria

4. Alice *Alicia is one variation.*

5. Allison *Also spelled Allyson. Alyssa is another option. Most people think of Allison as blonde and friendly.*

6. Amanda *She might go by Mandy.*

7. Amaya *A pretty Japanese name with a pretty meaning—"night rain."*

8. Amelia

9. Amy

10. Andrea

11. Angelina

12. Annika *Both a Russian and a Swedish name, and actually, I knew an Annika from Finland.*

13. Antonia

14. April *Abril is the Spanish version.*

15. Aria

16. Athena *The goddess of wisdom and war. Suitable for a brave, smart heroine.*

17. Audrey *I've always loved this name, which has an elegant association with Audrey Hepburn. Audra is a variation.*

18. Autumn

19. Bethany

20. Brandy

21. Bree *Irish in origin, this name is derived from the name Brigid.*

22. Bronwyn *This is a classic Welsh name.*

23. Brooke

24. Caitlin

25. Callista *This Greek name can also be spelled with a "k."*

26. Camille

27. Caprice *This seems like the name of someone who might get you into trouble, and it might be worth it.*

28. Carina *Also spelled Karina. Corinne is a similar name.*

29. Carissa

30. Caroline *Carrie is the most common nickname, and Carolina is a Spanish version. The Carolina I know has Colombian parents, and everyone calls her Caro.*

31. Catalina

32. Cecilia *Celia is a variation.*

33. Celeste

34. Chandra

35. Chantal *"Chantel" and "Shantell" are alternate spellings.*

36. Charlotte *"Lottie" is one possible nickname.*

37. Chaya *This is a Hebrew name meaning "life."*

38. Cherie

39. Chloe

40. Clara

41. Clio *This is the name of the muse of history—one of the nine muses in Greek mythology. Cleo is an alternate spelling.*

42. Colleen

43. Courtney

44. Daisy

45. Dalia *May also be spelled Dahlia, like the flower.*

46. Dana *Danae is a variation.*

47. Daphne

48. Dawn This is kind of an optimistic hippie name.

49. Delphine

50. Diamond

51. Diana

52. Devi *A Hindu name that means "divine" or "goddess."*

53. Dominique *A glamorous name of French origin. Monique has a similar feel.*

54. Eden

---

55. Elena *This is an Italian, Spanish, and eastern European version of Helen.*

56. Elise *Elyse is an alternate spelling.*

57. Elizabeth *All kinds of nicknames possible.*

58. Emily

59. Erin

60. Estelle *Stella is a variation.*

61. Eva *Could also be short for Evangeline.*

62. Faith

63. Felicia *Felicity is a variation.*

64. Fern

65. Florence *Flora or Flory are nice nicknames.*

66. Francesca

67. Gabriela *This is a Spanish name, and Gabriella and Gabrielle are English versions.*

68. Genevieve *Geneva is a similar choice.*

69. Georgia

70. Giselle

71. Grace

72. Haley *Can also be spelled Hayley.*

73. Hannah

74. Heidi

75. Holly

76. Hope

77. Imogene *This is an unusual but very classic name. It can also be spelled Imogen, but the "e" on the end helps with pronunciation.*

78. Ingrid *This Scandinavian name first got popular in the United States thanks to the actress Ingrid Bergman.*

79. Iris *A pretty flower and the name of a famous writer, Iris Murdoch.*

80. Ivy

81. Jacqueline* *Bound to have associations with elegance, thanks to Jackie Kennedy.*

82. Jade *People imagine that Jade has a carefree personality. Jada is a variation.*

83. Jamie.

84. Jamila *An Arabic name that means "beautiful." Can also be spelled Jamilla or Jamillah.*

85. Jane *I think of this as a good name for a reserved person, probably because of* Pride and Prejudice. *Janelle, Janine, and Janae are variants.*

86. Jasmine

87. Jennifer *Jenna is a variation.*

88. Jessamine *Jess or Jessie for short.*

89. Jia *A Chinese name that means "good" or "outstanding."*

90. Jillian *This could also be spelled Gillian.*

91. Joelle *This French name means "Jehovah is God."*

92. Jolene

93. Josephine *She could go by Jo, Joey, or Josie.*

94. Joy

95. Julia

96. June

97. Justine

98. Karen

99. Katherine *Also spelled Catherine, of course. There are a few different choices for nicknames here.*

100. Kelly

101. Kelsey *Can also be spelled Kelsie.*

102. Kendra

103. Kimberly *Also spelled Kimberley.*

104. Kristina

105. Lacey *Also spelled Lacy and Lacie.*

106. Lakeisha *Can also be spelled Lakesha.*

107. Laura *Lara is a popular variation.*

108. Lauren *Laurel is a similar choice.*

109. Leah

110. Leila *Layla is a possible alternate spelling.*

111. Lilly *Can also be spelled Lily if it's not short for Lillian.*

112. Lindsey *Can also be spelled Lindsay.*

113. Linnea

114. Lisa

115. London

116. Lucia

117. Lucy *Could be short for Lucille or Lucinda...or it might just be Lucy.*

118. Macy *Can also be spelled Macie or Macey.*

119. Maggie

120. Mara

121. Maria *As classic as it gets, and many people think of it as a Hispanic name.*

122. Marissa *Marisol is a similar option.*

123. Maureen

124. May

125. Maya

126. Megan

127. Melissa

128. Melody

129. Mercy

130. Millicent *I put this on here mostly because Millie is such a cute nickname.*

131. Mina *This name appears in a few different cultures, and in Bram Stroker's* Dracula.

132. Miranda

133. Molly *People think of Molly as really cute and maybe kind of innocent.*

134. Nadia

135. Naomi

136. Natalia *Or Natalie.*

137. Nicole

138. Nina

139. Noel *Also spelled Noelle.*

140. Octavia

141. Olivia

142. Oralie *This is a French name meaning "golden." Aurelia is a variation.*

143. Paige

144. Pamela

145. Pauline

146. Penelope *Although Penelope in* The Odyssey *stayed home and waited for twenty years, people imagine Penelope as an adventurous type. Lots of nickname options here: Pen, Penny, Nell, and Nellie.*

147. Phoebe

148. Piper

149. Poppy

150. Rae

151. Rachel *Also spelled Rachael.*

152. Rebecca *Frequently spelled "Rebekah."*

153. Renée

154. Rhiannon *This is the name of the Celtic goddess of horses, inspiration, and the moon. It's also a really old rock song.*

155. River *There are two terrific Rivers in science fiction: River Song in* Dr. Who *and River Tam in* Firefly.

156. Robin *An alternate spelling, Robyn, might seem more modern, but Robin Hood was often spelled "Robyn Hode."*

157. Rose

158. Rosemary

159. Rowan *"Rowena" is a variation.*

160. Roxanne *Roxy/Roxie is a pretty fun nickname.*

161. Ruby

162. Ruth

163. Samantha

164. Samara

165. Sarah *Frequently spelled without the final "h."*

166. Savannah *Sometimes spelled without the final "h."*

167. Selena *This is a version of Selene, the moon goddess of Greek mythology. Of course, the two big associations here are the late singer who went only by her first name, and Selena Gomez.*

168. Sasha

169. Serenity

170. Shasta

171. Shayla

172. Shea *Occasionally spelled Shay.*

173. Sidney *Might also be spelled Sydney.*

174. Simone

175. Skye

176. Sonia *Also spelled Sonya.*

177. Sophia *Sophronia is a similar but less common name. Sophie is short for either.*

178. Sylvia *Silvia is the Spanish and Italian version.*

179. Talia

180. Tameka *Aramaic in origin. Can also be spelled Tamika or Tamikah.*

181. Tara *People think of Tara as someone who likes to have fun.*

182. Tasha *Latasha is a variation.*

183. Tegan *Also spelled Teagan.*

184. Tessa *Or Tess. Either of these may be short for Theresa.*

185. Tia

186. Trinity

187. Valencia

188. Vanessa

189. Victoria

190. Vida

191. Viola

192. Violet

193. Virginia

194. Wendy

195. Winifred *She could go by Win, Winnie, Fred, or Freddie.*

196. Winter

197. Wren

198. Zara *This can also be spelled Zahra.*

199. Zephyr

200. Zoe

200 NAMES FOR CONTEMPORARY HEROES

I originally developed a shorter version of this list with the romance fiction genre in mind, but this expanded version can be used for all kinds of leading men in any genre. Again, I have emphasized names that are popular in the United States for men in their 20s, 30s, and 40s, but I've included unusual names as well. I hope you find one that's just perfect for your guy!

1. Aaron

2. Adam *Quintessential solid good-guy name.*

3. Aidan *Can also be spelled Aiden.*

4. Alaric *Also spelled Alarik.*

5. Alden

6. Alexander *He can go by Alex or Xander.*

7. Amir *This is both of Arabic and of Hebrew origin.*

8. Andrew *Andreas is a popular version in Germany.*

9. Arturo *Arthur is the English version.*

10. Asher *Ashton is a similar name. Either one could go by Ash.*

11. August

12. Aziel *I was sure this would be the name of a Biblical angel or demon, but no.*

13. Blake

14. Benedict *A variation, Benedick, appears in Shakespeare's* As You Like It.

15. Benjamin

16. Bowie

17. Bradford

18. Brady

19. Brandon

20. Brian *Brion and Bryan are alternate spellings.*

21. Brody

22. Bruce *The actor Bruce Willis and the comic book character Bruce Wayne are two strong associations here.*

23. Bryce

24. Burne *May also be spelled Byrne.*

25. Byron *Maybe for a hero who is, like the famous poet, "mad, bad, and dangerous to know."*

26. Caleb

27. Cameron

28. Campbell

29. Carrick

30. Carter

31. Chance

32. Charles *Several nicknames are possible. You might prefer the Spanish version, Carlos.*

33. Chase

34. Christopher

35. Clayton *Or just Clay.*

36. Cole

37. Colt *He's tough! Like a gun! But vulnerable! Like a baby horse! His full name might be Colton.*

38. Clark *Famous Clarks include Clark Kent and Clark Gable.*

39. Clive

40. Conall *This Irish name means "strong in battle."*

41. Connor

42. Craig

43. Daire

44. Dalton

45. Dane

46. Daniel

47. Dante *Because of* The Inferno, *people will likely see this hero as brooding or dangerous.*

48. Darius

49. David

50. Dax *It's an unusual name, but it pops up in the U.S. now and again.*

51. Dean

52. Denver

53. Derek

54. Desmond

55. Dimitri *This name is Greek in origin, and also popular in Russia. Demetrius is a variation.*

56. Dominic *Also spelled Dominick or Domenic.*

57. Donovan

58. Dorran *This is a Celtic name that means "stranger."*

59. Dougal *Also spelled Dougall.*

60. Dylan

61. Edward *Eduardo is the Spanish version.*

62. Elijah *Elijahs frequently go by Eli.*

63. Elliot *Can also be spelled Elliott. Ellison is a similar name.*

64. Ephraim

65. Eric *The spelling Erik is more Scandinavian, and somehow looks more daring.*

66. Ethan

67. Eugene

68. Evan

69. Ezra *This Hebrew name means "helper."*

70. Finn

71. Ford

72. Frederick

73. Gabriel

74. Gage

75. Gareth *This is the name of one of the Knights of the Round Table.*

76. Garrett

77. Gerard

78. Gideon *This Biblical name has a pretty serious sound to it.*

79. Glen

80. Grady

81. Grant

82. Gregory

83. Griffin *He's named after a mythological beast, so that automatically makes him awesome.*

84. Henry *Nicknames for Henry, weirdly enough, include Hal and Hank.*

85. Harry

86. Harris

87. Hudson

88. Hunter

89. Ian *One of the most famous Ians is Ian Fleming, the writer who created James Bond.*

90. Irving

91. Isaiah

92. Issac

93. Ivan

94. Jack *Sometimes a nickname for John or Jonathan. Of course, it's also short for Jackson, and you might want to use that full name.*

95. Jake *Probably short for Jacob.*

96. Jamal

97. James

98. Jared *I've also seen it spelled Jarrod and Jerrod.*

99. Jason

100. Javier *This is a great Spanish name.*

101. Jay *Famous Jays include Jay Gatsby and Jay-Z.*

102. Jeremy

103. Jericho

104. Jesse

105. John *The quintessential everyman name. Jonathan is an alternative.*

106. Joel

107. Joshua

108. Julian *Some people feel that this name sounds a little feminine or unisex. I don't agree, and I don't think that's a bad thing, anyway.*

109. Justin

110. Kane

111. Kendrick

112. Kento *This is a pretty cool name for your Japanese or Japanese-American hero.*

113. Kevin

114. Kingsley

115. Kirk

116. Kyle

117. Lance *Or you could just go ahead and name him Lancelot.*

118. Landon

119. Leo *Sometimes this is short for Leonardo, and sometimes it's not.*

120. Li *This super-popular Chinese name means "strength."*

121. Liam

122. Lincoln

123. Lionel

124. Locke

125. Logan

126. Lorenzo *This is an Italian and Spanish version of Lawrence that most people find really sexy.*

127. Louis *Famous Louises include all those French kings, and Louis Armstrong.*

128. Lucas

129. Luke

130. Luther *This German name means "famous warrior," but people imagine Luther as being more of a quiet type.*

131. Maddox

132. Malachi

133. Malik *This is an Arabic name meaning "lord," "ruler," or "chief."*

134. Marcus *Or simply Marc.*

135. Marshall

136. Matthew* *Chances are good that most people call him Matt. Mathias is an alternative, and Mateo is the Spanish version.*

137. Mason

138. Max *Could be short for Maxim, Maxwell, or Maximilian.*

139. Micah

140. Michael* *Mikhail is a Russian variation.*

141. Miles

142. Monty *This is generally short for Montgomery.*

143. Morgan

144. Nathan* *This could be short for Nathaniel. Either Nathan or Nathaniel could go by Nate.*

---

145. Neal

146. Nicholas*

147. Noah

148. Oliver

149. Orion *This is the name of a constellation, which in turn takes its name from a legendary hunter in Greek mythology.*

150. Orlando

151. Owen

152. Patrick*

153. Paul

154. Pavel *This is a fairly popular Russian name.*

155. Peter*

156. Pierce *Piers is an alternative.*

157. Quinn

158. Ramon

159. Raphael *This is the name of an archangel in Hebrew tradition, and also the name of one of the most famous painters of the Italian Renaissance. Rafael is the Spanish version.*

160. Raine

161. Reed *Can also be spelled Reid.*

162. Roan

163. Roark *Can also be spelled Roarke.*

164. Robert

165. Roderick

166. Roger *Also spelled Rodger.*

167. Roland *This is a very cool old German name that shows up in Shakespeare. It seems like no one ever uses it. Rollo is the typical nickname.*

168. Richard

169. Ryan

170. Ryder *He's going to come off as something of a cowboy, whether he is one or not.*

171. Samuel* *Almost all Samuels go by Sam.*

172. Sean* *Can also be spelled Shawn or Shaun.*

173. Seth

174. Simon

175. Spencer

176. Stephen *Stefan is a popular variation of German origin.*

177. Tariq *A name of Arabic origin, also spelled Tarek or Tarik.*

178. Tavis *Tavish is a variation.*

179. Terrence

180. Theodore *He might go by Ted, Teddy, or Theo.*

181. Thomas* *The nickname Tom is more no-nonsense, while Thomas is fancier.*

182. Timothy* *Most Timothys go by Tim.*

183. Travis*

184. Tremaine

185. Trenton *Or just Trent. Almost everyone seems to have positive associations with this name.*

186. Trevor

187. Trey *This Latin name means "three" or "third."*

188. Tristan

189. Vance

190. Vaughn

191. Victor *I love how this name is a synonym for "winner."*

192. Vincent

193. Wade

194. Ward

195. Weston *This is a good name for a rich jerk, who might turn out to be not a jerk at all. For a more down-to-earth variation, just go with West.*

196. William* *The nicknames Bill, Billy, and William each have a very different feel.*

197. Wyatt *Another cowboy-type name.*

198. Xavier

199. Zach* *Short for Zachary or Zachariah. If you want something not so American, you could go with Zak, short for Zakhar, which is a Russian name.*

200. Zane *Zain is an alternate spelling.*

100 VERY COMMON LAST NAMES IN THE U.S. TODAY

Need a popular last name for an American character? Pick one from here! Many of these are very common in Canada, the U.K., and Australia as well. The names marked with an asterisk are the ten most common names in the U.S., according to the 2010 census.

Adams	Allen	Anderson	Bailey
Baker	Barnes	Bell	Bennett
Brooks	Brown*	Butler	Campbell
Carter	Clark	Coleman	Collins
Cook	Cooper	Cox	Cruz
Davis*	Diaz	Edwards	Evans
Foster	Garcia*	Gomez	Gonzalez
Gray	Green	Gutierrez	Fisher
Flores	Hall	Harris	Henderson
Hernandez	Hill	Howard	Hughes
Jackson	James	Jenkins	Johnson*
Jones*	Kelly	King	Lee
Lewis	Long	Lopez	Martin
Martinez	Miller*	Mitchell	Moore

Morales	Morgan	Morris	Murphy
Myers	Nguyen	Ortiz	Parker
Perry	Peterson	Phillips	Perez
Powell	Price	Reed	Reyes
Richardson	Rivera	Roberts	Robinson
Rodriguez*	Rogers	Ross	Russell
Sanchez	Sanders	Scott	Smith*
Stewart	Sullivan	Taylor	Thomas
Thompson	Torres	Turner	Walker
Ward	Watson	White	Williams*
Wilson*	Wood	Wright	Young

7. CHARACTER TRAITS

Sometimes we get the idea for a story before we have a clue about the characters in it. Even when characters spring into our imaginations, we don't usually know everything about them at first. What do they do for a living? What's their history? What are they into? Basically, what makes them tick?

I heard a writer say once that most stories are about blood and money—people's families, and how they make a living. While some stories don't involve these elements, they are good things to figure out for your characters.

Even if your character is basically good, he or she will need flaws in order to be believable. Likewise, a good villain may have some admirable traits.

In addition to the lists in this section, two previous lists may help in thinking about the people in your story: the "Master List of Physical Descriptions," and "50 Goals and Aspirations." With careful thought, you can create a character who is as real in your readers' minds as anyone else they know in real life... a character they will never forget.

100 POSITIVE CHARACTER TRAITS

What are some of the strengths that your character relies on when the going gets tough? What's her everyday superpower? Here are lots of possibilities! In some cases, I've given an example or two of how they might play out, but of course that will depend on your story.

1. Accountable.

   He takes responsibility for his actions.

2. Active.

   She loves biking, hiking, gardening, or volunteering. She's not so into sitting around and watching TV.

3. Adventurous.

   Dodgy vacation destinations and big changes in her life don't scare her. She's always up for something new.

4. Affectionate.

   You can always count on him for a hug, a kind word, or good-natured teasing.

5. Agreeable.

   You want to go to a hockey game? She says, Sure, that sounds fine. No, wait, you want to go to a cooking class instead? Okay, she says, sounds good.

6. Ambitious.

   He has goals and dreams, and he's positive he can achieve them.

7. Appreciative.

   She shows gratitude for small favors and doesn't take any of her blessings for granted.

8. Articulate.

   She's rarely at a loss for words. Her comments and speeches are on point.

9. Artistic.

   He has a flair for painting, sculpting, photography, or design.

10. Balanced.

    Her life is evenly divided between work and play.

11. Brave.

    He might be scared, or he might not be. It doesn't matter. If there's a good reason to do the scary thing, he does it.

12. Capable.

    He's competent and can handle situations and tasks successfully.

13. Charismatic.

    It may be hard to say why, but she just has a glow that attracts people to her.

14. Chivalrous.

    He treats women with old-fashioned politeness and gallantry.

15. Cheerful.

    On a regular day, he whistles while he works and never stops smiling. Even in tough times, he finds some reason to be happy.

16. Compassionate.

    His heart goes out to those in distress, and he does what he can to help.

17. Confident.

    She believes in her value and the quality of her work.

18. Considerate.

He remembers your kids' names, and even your dog's name. When you miss class, he grabs an extra handout for you.

19. Cooperative.

Group project? No problem. She excels at working with others.

20. Cultured.

He can tell you about theater, the history of jazz, and every little gallery in town.

21. Curious.

She wants to learn about everyone and everything.

22. Cute.

It's not just the way she looks, but the whimsical and guileless way she dresses and acts that makes her adorable.

23. Decisive.

He doesn't waste a bunch of time trying to figure out a course of action. He chooses to do something, and he does it. Bam. End of story. (Or possibly, the beginning of the story.)

24. Dependable.

She never shirks her responsibilities.

25. Dignified.

His self-respect shines through his words, gestures, and the way he presents himself.

26. Disciplined.

He exerts self-control to meet his goals.

27. Discreet.

She can keep a secret, or a hundred of them.

28. Easygoing.

She's relaxed, slow to get upset, and rarely takes offense.

29. Efficient.

He gets things done quickly, in the simplest way possible.

30. Empathetic.

He understands how people feel and why they do what they do.

31. Empowering.

She makes others feel like they can do just about anything.

32. Energetic.

As long as he gets his required five hours of sleep a night, he keeps going and going.

33. Enthusiastic.

She gets excited about plans, events, and occasions.

34. Entrepreneurial.

She has great ideas for new businesses, and the drive to see them through.

35. Fair.

He tries to make sure that no one gets shortchanged.

36. Faithful.

She's committed to her spouse, and doesn't even flirt with anyone else.

37. Family-oriented.

His spouse and kids come before everything else.

38. Flamboyant.

He lives out loud and does everything in a big way. This may be more of a neutral than a positive trait.

39. Flexible.

She can change her routine or her usual way of working to suit the situation.

40. Friendly.

She goes out of her way to connect with others.

41. Frugal.

She saves 15% of every paycheck, re-uses plastic sandwich bags, and never has to toss vegetables that are past their prime.

42. Funny.

He always has something hilarious to say.

43. Generous.

If you need twenty bucks or you want half of his cookie, he'll say yes.

44. Gentle.

She has a soft, caring manner, and would never hurt anyone.

45. Good Listener.

He doesn't just think about the next thing he will say. He actually pays attention.

46. Good Teacher.

She knows how to explain things and encourage people as they learn.

47. Graceful.

He carries himself in an elegant way.

48. Handy.

She knows how to fix things around the house.

49. Health-conscious.

She works out, eats right, and gets enough sleep.

50. Honest.

He never takes what isn't his, and he's always truthful.

51. Honorable.

He doesn't take advantage of others, and he's always good for his word.

52. Idealistic.

She has hopes for a healthier planet or a better society.

53. Imaginative.

She can see possibilities where others cannot, and can invent elaborate stories or worlds.

54. Independent.

He doesn't mind eating alone in a restaurant. If no one else shares his opinion on something, he's fine with that.

55. Industrious.

She's not afraid of a little hard work. In fact, she's not afraid of a lot of hard work.

56. Innocent.

Although this trait can get people into trouble, it's often charming.

57. Intelligent.

She learns things and solves problems quickly.

58. Intuitive.

His hunches often prove correct, and he knows when something's off. It could be a slightly supernatural talent, or he might just synthesize a lot of disparate data on a subconscious level.

59. Knowledgeable.

He's an expert in his field, or in many fields.

60. Lighthearted.

She's quick to laugh at a joke, and finds many things pleasant or amusing.

61. Logical.

Instead of letting emotions or fears take over, she looks at the facts.

62. Loyal.

He's true to his family, his friends, and his company.

63. Meticulous.

She makes sure all the small details are correct.

64. Modest.

He doesn't draw attention to himself or his achievements, and doesn't especially want others too, either.

65. Mysterious.

Her enigmatic appearance, words, or behavior intrigue or confuse people. This can be a neutral rather than a positive trait.

66. Natural Leader.

Others look to her for direction, because she's skilled at giving it.

67. Nature-loving.

He has a strong connection with animals, trees, and the great outdoors.

68. Neat.

He's well groomed, and he keeps his apartment and even his car tidy.

69. Nurturing.

She instinctively takes care of others and makes them feel loved.

70. Observant.

He notices and recalls small details that most people miss.

71. Organized.

She has a system for everything.

72. Optimistic.

She always expects the best-case scenario.

73. Passionate.

He feels things deeply, and expresses them emphatically.

74. Patient.

She doesn't get frustrated when something or someone takes a long time.

75. Peace-making.

Not only does he avoid fighting himself, but he also tries to keep others from doing it.

76. Persuasive.

She could sell bikinis in Antarctica.

77. Polite.

Even in strained or unusual situations, her manners serve her well.

78. Punctual.

He never apologizes for being late, because he never needs to.

79. Quiet.

This is actually neither a positive nor a negative trait, but it had to go somewhere.

80. Resourceful.

He can cook a delicious meal out of the most random remains in the kitchen cupboard, or build a comfortable living shelter out of trash he found in an alley.

81. Restrained.

Even if she's jealous, hurt, or angry, she doesn't throw a fit.

82. Romantic.

Thoughtful gifts, sweet nothings, and grand gestures of love are his "thing."

83. Scholarly.

She feels most at home in the classroom or the library.

84. Serene.

He may be facing certain death, or even his toddler's meltdown, but he keeps his cool.

85. Sexy.

Not just his looks, but his words and gestures are enticing.

86. Shrewd.

His good judgment helps him strike favorable bargains and deals.

87. Spiritual.

She has a deep connection with God, nature, or something else larger than herself.

88. Spontaneous.

She can drop everything she's doing if an interesting plan presents itself.

89. Stylish.

Her clothing choices and maybe the interior of her home show real flair.

90. Suave.

He has a polished charm that serves him well in social situations.

91. Tactful.

He avoids awkward questions and preserves other people's privacy and dignity.

92. Tech-savvy.

When people have computer questions, he's the one they call.

93. Tenacious.

Her first plan didn't work? Plan B didn't either? That's fine. She doesn't just have a Plan C—she has the whole alphabet and then some. She's not giving up.

94. Tolerant.

She won't complain about the empty wine bottles you left around the kitchen or make fun of your conviction that you were abducted by aliens. "Live and let live" is stamped into her very soul.

95. Tough.

Despite pain or adversity, he doesn't complain and he doesn't quit.

96. Unpretentious.

She doesn't share perfectly filtered photos on social media, or try to impress everybody at the party. She's honest about herself and her life, and it's refreshing.

97. Vivacious.

His warm, talkative manner makes people feel good.

98. Wise.

People naturally look to her for advice, and she steers them in the right direction.

99. Youthful.

He does things that you would never expect someone his age to do.

100. Zany.

She's a nut. There's never a dull moment around her. This is another one that could be negative, but I think it's most often a good thing.

100 NEGATIVE CHARACTER TRAITS

Even the nicest character has his weaknesses. If he doesn't, nobody's going to like him that much – paradoxical, maybe, but true. Your nastier characters may have a whole suite of bad qualities, or they may have one that people find unforgivable.

Some of these qualities may not be things your characters can really help or change. These may make things difficult for your characters, but they are not moral failures.

1. Absent-minded.

   She has no idea where she left her papers, and she forgot about her meeting. She just can't seem to get it together.

2. Aggressive.

   Whether she's on the interstate or in a conversation, she's confrontational for no very good reason.

3. Aloof.

   He's so chilly, you need a sweater to go near him.

4. Antisocial.

   He rarely wants to take part in a conversation, let alone a friendly meal or a party.

5. Anxious.

   Certain situations make her nervous—or maybe it's life in general.

6. Apathetic.

   She doesn't take an interest in others' lives, and her own life bores her even more.

7. Argumentative.

The devil never had a better advocate than this guy. Sometimes he argues just to be contrary.

8. Authoritarian.

She bosses people around and tries to dictate their words and actions. Nobody had better make a move without her approval.

9. Awkward.

Although he means well, he has a knack for saying the wrong thing at the wrong time.

10. Bitter.

He feels he was treated unfairly, and he will never, ever get over it.

11. Brusque.

He seems to think talking to others is a waste of time.

12. Callous.

When she sees those sad commercials about abused cats and dogs, she doesn't even sniffle. The plight of others leaves her unmoved.

13. Careless.

If she hasn't been in a car accident lately, she's probably caused one.

14. Childish.

She expects immediate gratification and has a meltdown when she doesn't get it. She's a 3-year-old trapped in an adult body.

15. Clumsy.

He's always dropping things or running into things.

16. Conceited.

It's a wonder her ego can get through doorways.

17. Condescending.

How kind of her to deign to explain things to you.

18. Commitment-phobic.

He can't promise to show up at a barbecue, let alone promise to be faithful.

19. Conformist.

If all of his friends jumped off a cliff, he would do it, too, while telling everyone he's always been into cliff diving.

20. Cowardly.

She runs from even the hint of danger or risk.

21. Cruel.

Another person's pain amuses him...so much so, in fact, that he'll often cause it. This is a flaw that readers find very hard to forgive.

22. Cynical.

She greets even positive situations with a jaded attitude.

23. Delusional.

He has grandiose ideas about himself and expectations for his life. This is only a negative thing when it starts to harm how he relates to others or how he pursues opportunities.

24. Demanding.

As a boss, a parent, or a lover, she has a long list of things she expects you to do.

25. Dependent.

He's clingy, and he can't stand on his own two feet.

26. Depressed.

It may not be his fault that he's sad all the time, but it does make it difficult on everyone else.

27. Dishonest.

He lies whenever it suits him, and he steals if he can get away with it.

28. Disloyal.

It doesn't matter how much you've been through together or how much she owes you. She'll turn on you if it benefits her.

29. Drama-loving.

He might say, "I don't want any drama," but he thrives on conflict, and his words and actions stir it up.

30. Dull.

She has no particular interests and no strong feelings. She does the same things every day. She's just boring. (Readers will also have a hard time forgiving this in a main character.)

31. Foolish.

She makes terrible decisions on a fairly regular basis.

32. Frivolous.

He wastes time and money on meaningless pursuits.

33. Fussy.

The layout of a document, temperature in a car...everything has to be "just so" for this person.

34. Gossipy.

She always passes on juicy stories, whether they're true or not.

35. Grouchy.

Complaining about the weather is his way of saying "good morning."

36. Gullible.

You can draw her into almost any scheme or bad situation.

37. Harsh.

His words, lessons, or punishments are needlessly severe.

38. Hedonistic.

He indulges himself and puts his immediate pleasure above pretty much everything else.

39. Hot-tempered.

It's not hard to set her off, and she yells a lot.

40. Hypercritical.

As far as she's concerned, every flaw is worth mentioning, or even discussing in detail.

41. Hypocritical.

For instance, she holds forth on the sanctity of marriage, and she's having an affair.

42. Ignorant.

He doesn't know much about the world. If he is willing to learn, it's forgivable. If he prefers to stay ignorant, it's not.

43. Impatient.

Waiting just about kills him, and he lets everybody know.

44. Indecisive.

It takes her so long to choose a restaurant that by the time she does, they're all closed for the night. For years, she's been trying to decide whether or not she should leave her husband or go back to school.

45. Inflexible.

He doesn't want to change his plans or routines for any reason.

46. Inhibited.

She can't loosen up and be herself.

47. Insecure.

He requires a lot of reassuring and flattering, and he often has the need to prove that he measures up to others.

48. Interfering.

It may be none of her business, but she'll make it her business.

49. Intolerant.

People who are different from her frankly infuriate her.

50. Irrational.

He makes decisions based on fleeting emotions or ridiculous fancies rather than reasonable considerations.

51. Jealous.

She fumes over the fact that other people have nice boyfriends, lovely homes, or good jobs, when she doesn't. It's just not fair!

52. Judgmental.

Who died and left him God? Apparently he thinks *somebody* did.

53. Lazy.

Her life would be so much better if she could just get motivated.

54. Lecherous.

He hits on people constantly, regardless of whether they seem interested or not.

55. Loud.

This is not always a negative character trait, but it certainly can be annoying in some situations.

56. Manipulative.

She finds sneaky ways to get other people to do what she wants.

57. Materialistic.

His prime concern is to acquire more and better stuff than anyone else.

58. Messy.

His room, his truck, his hair, or all of the above are a disaster.

59. Moody.

She is fine one minute and moping the next.

60. Narrow-minded.

She won't listen to other points of view.

61. Obsequious.

He could care less about people of lower social standing, but he sucks up to important people.

62. Obsessive.

She just can't let something go.

63. Opposed to change.

New procedures, circumstances, technology and trends threaten him.

64. Overcommitted.

She always takes on more than she can handle.

65. Overtalkative.

It's hard to get a word in edgewise.

66. Passive.

Maybe he doesn't do anything evil, but he doesn't do anything to stop it, either.

67. Pedantic.

She belabors all the details and formalities.

68. Perverted.

He has disturbing inclinations.

69. Pessimistic.

She always expects the worst-case scenario, which is much worse than anything you could have imagined.

70. Petty.

He gets hung up on the slightest of slights.

71. Pompous.

She's self-important and pretentious.

72. Possessive.

He acts like his wife or girlfriend is his private property.

73. Prickly.

You never know what will offend him.

74. Procrastinating.

She puts everything off until the last minute.

75. Proud.

She doesn't ask for or accept help, even when it's the most sensible thing to do.

76. Pseudo-intellectual.

He takes every opportunity to pretend he is well read or highly philosophical.

77. Rebellious.

This can be a positive trait, but only if there's a good reason for it.

78. Rude.

Where are his manners? Nowhere to be found.

79. Sanctimonious.

Why can't everyone live up to her high moral standards? That's all she wants to know.

80. Self-centered.

She will rarely ask herself how her actions or a situation will affect anyone else but her.

81. Shallow.

He's almost incapable of considering or discussing weighty matters.

82. Shy.

He won't strike up a conversation and will get nervous if you do.

83. Smug.

Her life is perfect, and she will be the first to tell you that this is all because of her good choices.

84. Snobbish.

If you invite her to dinner, she'll turn her nose up at your bargain wine or your grandma's fried chicken recipe.

85. Stingy.

Waitresses hate him.

86. Stubborn.

Trying to get her to change her mind on anything is close to impossible.

87. Suspicious.

He's pretty sure everyone's out to get him...so much so, you kind of hope that somebody does.

88. Tacky.

She's too loud, she dresses inappropriately, and she has no social graces.

89. Unable to Admit Mistakes.

Even when it's clear that he messed up, he'll have some kind of story or excuse.

90. Undisciplined.

She can't stick to a plan or exert much self-control.

91. Ungrateful.

His grandma paid for some of his college. He can't even be bothered to send her a birthday card.

92. Unimaginative.

She can't envision other possibilities.

93. Vain.

He's attractive, sure...especially in that big oil painting of himself hanging over his mantel. However, he isn't nearly as handsome as he thinks he is.

94. Vindictive.

If she thinks she's been wronged, she will try to even the score and then some.

95. Violent.

She handles disagreements by breaking dishes or breaking bones.

96. Vulgar.

He makes inappropriate and gross jokes. He makes his bodily functions everybody's business.

97. Wasteful.

He doesn't just spend money on things he doesn't really need…he spends money on things that nobody on earth needs.

98. Weak.

When the going gets tough, she lies down and gives up.

99. Workaholic.

He can't make time for his partner, his family, his friends, or anything else.

100. Whiny.

Not only does he complain a lot, but he does it in an annoying tone of voice.

25 POSITIVE CHARACTER TRAITS
THAT CAN ALSO BE NEGATIVE

When you were reading through the lists of positive character traits, did you find yourself thinking, "Well, that one can be annoying at times"? And in the list of negative character traits, did you ever think, "Hey, that's not always a bad thing?"

One key to creating great characters is to give them strengths that are *also* flaws. Here are 25 examples of personal qualities...and how they can sometimes be too much of a good thing.

1. **The good quality:** He wants to protect everyone he cares about, plus anyone else he perceives as needing protection.

   How it can be bad: He may boss people around too much—for their own good, in his mind. To repel a threat, he might use more force than necessary, and he might even perceive a threat where there isn't one.

2. **The good quality:** She's an optimist. Even in tough circumstances, she looks on the bright side, which makes her a cheerful person.

   How it can be bad: When people feel angry, sad, or discouraged, she may make things worse by telling them to cheer up. She may pursue grand plans that don't have a chance of working.

3. **The good quality:** He has a great sense of humor. For any situation, he has a hilarious comment.

   How it can be bad: He might joke about things that really aren't that funny, and be unable to discuss something seriously. His wisecracks may wind up exposing people's vulnerabilities and hurting their feelings.

4. **The good quality:** She has a lot of self-discipline. Sticking to a workout schedule and finishing a difficult project are no problem for her.

How it can be bad: Trying to get her to abandon her routine, even for a good reason, may be next to impossible. She may not know how to relax and have fun.

5. **The good quality**: He loves new experiences and adapts easily even to abrupt changes in circumstances.

   How it can be bad: In stable, predictable environments, he gets bored and restless. He might abandon people or responsibilities entirely.

6. **The good quality:** She's agreeable and goes along with plans, never starting arguments or causing conflicts. This makes her a great team member and a favorite employee.

   How it can be bad: She carries out orders even if they are immoral or illegal. She'll be the first person to say later that she was just doing her job.

7. **The good quality:** He's sensitive to other people's feelings. He frequently shows and tells his family and friends how much he loves them.

   How it can be bad: He may take things very personally, even when they weren't intended that way. At times, he may be too clingy.

8. **The good quality:** She has charisma to spare. People are naturally drawn to her company and conversation.

   How it can be bad: She might always demand to be the center of attention, even when it's somebody else's turn.

9. **The good quality:** He is meticulous. His email inbox is always cleaned out, his apartment is always immaculate, and he's the only one to read the fine print.

   How it can be bad: He might think everyone should organize things the same way he does, and he might be so fussy and critical that he drives everybody nuts.

10. **The good quality:** She is ambitious. So far, she's made her own way in the world, and she is just getting started.

    How it can be bad: She might be ruthless in pursuing her goals. In order to win, she might be willing to cheat, lie, or manipulate others.

11. **The good quality:** He is a creative genius. His paintings, movies, or books enthrall people.

    How it can be bad: He may struggle with depression, anxiety, or other mental health issues, and he may resist treatment because he's afraid it will alter his work.

12. **The good quality:** She's candid and honest about her opinions and her own mistakes. It's refreshing.

    How it can be bad: She might not be able to keep her mouth shut, even when that would be the best course of action. Her words may make people feel bad or get her and everybody else into trouble.

13. **The good quality:** He's an idealist. A humanitarian, he works and campaigns to make the world a better place.

    How it can be bad: There may be no middle ground for him—he won't settle for anything less than his vision. As lofty as his ideals for humanity are, he might not be kind to individual people.

14. **The good quality:** She has a great imagination. She can get lost in books and TV shows, and she's a good storyteller herself.

    How it can be bad: She might be an escapist who avoids real-life problems and responsibilities. She may not engage enough with the real people around her.

15. **The good quality:** He has impeccable taste. In clothing, interiors, music, or all of the above, he's knowledgeable and has true style.

    How it can be bad: His high level of taste may lead him to overspend. He may look down on those with less refined sensibilities.

16. **The good quality:** Her analytical skills are beyond compare. She can look at the facts objectively and propose rational solutions.

    How it can be bad: She may fail to understand when someone just wants empathy rather than a practical solution. She might not be that great at expressing warm feelings in general.

17. **The good quality:** He's outgoing and gregarious. His social calendar is full, and he has friends everywhere.

    How it can be bad: He may have no idea how to entertain himself and might not deal well with solitude. He may not be a deep thinker.

18. **The good quality:** She's strong and stoic. Even when things get really tough, she doesn't complain.

    How it can be bad: She might expect everyone else to be just as tough as she is and fail to show much pity.

19. **The good quality:** He's a very sensual person. He knows how to take great pleasure in good food, sex, and other indulgences.

    How it can be bad: He may overindulge, leading to addictive behavior. Alternately, he may be selfish, putting his gratification above other people's feelings.

20. **The good quality:** She's confident. In every situation, she believes in herself and her abilities, and that assurance often leads other people to trust her as well.

    How it can be bad: She may not ask for advice, even when she doesn't know what she is doing and could really use it.

21. **The good quality:** He takes care of his health. He works out, eats right, and reads articles about nutrition.

    How it can be bad: He may lecture other people about their choices, and he may treat unhealthiness as a moral failing.

22. **The good quality:** She is a strong critical thinker. She can see through propaganda and recognize when an argument doesn't hold up.

   How it can be bad: She might be too critical and negative, and she might over-analyze everything.

23. **The good quality:** He's conscientious, and he obeys rules to the letter of the law.

   How it can be bad: He may want to punish others for harmless infractions, or enforce rules that make no sense.

24. **The good quality:** She's prudent. Before taking action, she researches the matter and weighs the possible consequences.

   How it can be bad: If she's overwhelmed with data, she might be unable to make a decision. Even in dire circumstances, she may be unable to take quick action.

25. **The good quality:** He's humble and modest. You'll never hear him bragging about anything.

   How it can be bad: He may not ever live up to his potential, and he may deprive the world of his unique gifts.

50 PAST TRAUMAS

One of my favorite poets, Robert Hass, began his poem "Meditation at Lagunitas" with these lines: "All the new thinking is about loss./In this it resembles all the old thinking."

Nobody gets through life without tragedies. Sometimes we forget how ubiquitous they are, because people don't always discuss them. The most successful, attractive, popular, and competent people still have heartbreak in their pasts.

The difficulties your character faced in the past may or may not play a large role in your story. Either way, they will affect her personality and the way she deals with immediate challenges.

Although I made this list with backstories in mind, you may find inspiration here for a main plot.

The items on this list range from upsetting to seriously damaging— and of course, different characters would respond differently to any of them. They are in no particular order. I have not elaborated on some of the worst things because I want to avoid triggering strong negative emotional responses in people who have experienced them in the past.

A character's past trauma may affect her in many different ways. She may be unwilling to try or take risks in some area of her life. She may lack confidence or self-esteem. It may have resulted in a low-level depression, marked by listlessness, aches and pains, insomnia, or chronic fatigue.

If she has post-traumatic stress disorder, she may experience bad dreams or flashbacks about the event. When something reminds her of it, her heartbeat and her breathing may accelerate with panic.

You may shy away from giving the people in your story real problems, but unfortunately, making life perfect for your characters rarely results in an interesting story. No matter how awful your character's past is, you can write her into healing and a much brighter future. Her story may provide just the inspiration a reader needed.

1. She was fired from a job.

   Maybe she didn't see it coming, or maybe she did and was unable to stop it. Either way, this can be a body blow.

2. His partner cheated on him.

   This could raise feelings of inadequacy, anger, and profound distrust in future relationships.

3. Her best friend betrayed her.

   This can hurt almost as much as the betrayal of a lover, and people around her might not understand that.

4. He was molested as a child.

5. She was sexually assaulted or raped as an adult.

6. His parent abandoned the family when he was young.

7. She was bullied as a child.

   She might have been singled out for ridicule because of her appearance, her learning style, or her behavior.

8. One or both of his parents or a sibling died when he was young.

9. One of her parents or a sibling died recently.

10. His spouse died recently.

11. Her dog or cat died recently.

    Not everyone recognizes how much grief this can actually cause, which may make things all the more difficult.

12. He made an accidental but catastrophic mistake.

    For instance, he might have run over someone's dog.

13. She was scammed out of a bunch of money.

14. He was mugged or robbed.

15. She was injured in sports or in a bad accident.

16. He was rejected from the college he always dreamed of attending.

17. She didn't get the chance to go to college at all.

    Maybe she really wanted to, but it wasn't possible because of her grades, finances, or a family situation.

18. He failed out of college, or was unable to finish.

    Mental health issues, a family crisis, or financial circumstances may have been to blame.

19. She got pregnant as a teen.

    Whether she terminated the pregnancy, had the baby and gave it up for adoption, or chose to become a mother, she may have been shamed about her pregnancy and her decision.

20. She suffered a miscarriage.

    Others may make it worse by saying it was God's plan or that she can get pregnant again.

21. He was demoted at work.

22. His new venture failed.

    It's not only disappointing, but also embarrassing.

23. She was physically abused as a child.

24. He was emotionally abused as a child.

25. As an adult, she was physically or emotionally abused by a partner.

26. His father physically abused his mother.

27. She was arrested.

28. He went to prison.

29. Her parent went to prison.

30. His spouse divorced him, or his boyfriend moved out with little warning.

31. Her fiancé called off the wedding.

    Alternately, he simply didn't show up for the ceremony.

32. He was evicted from his apartment.

33. She suffered a public embarrassment.

    She might have fallen on her butt in front of a huge crowd, or she might have been in an embarrassing video that went viral.

34. He lost access to his children.

    Maybe he was deported, or maybe his ex disappeared with them.

35. She witnessed a horrific accident or violent crime.

36. He fought in a war.

37. She or someone close to her was the victim of police brutality.

38. As a child, he was indoctrinated into a cult or religious sect with damaging beliefs.

39. As a child, she lived in poverty.

    She might have often lacked adequate food, decent clothes, or other necessities.

40. He survived a hurricane, plane crash, or other disaster.

41. She was very ill as a child or teen.

    Extensive treatment or surgeries early in life may have had a lasting impact.

42. He survived a serious illness as an adult.

43. The person he loved married somebody else.

44. She learned some shocking news about herself or her family.

45. At a school or workplace, she was harassed for her race or sexual orientation.

46. When she came out as a lesbian, family members or friends rejected her.

47. He lost his license or accreditation.

He might be a lawyer who was disbarred, a doctor who lost his medical license, or a priest who was defrocked.

48. She lived in an unsafe place.

It may have been in a high-crime area or in a war zone.

49. He lost something important.

He may have misplaced a winning lottery ticket or the heirloom diamond ring he was going to use when he proposed to his girlfriend.

50. She lost the respect of the person whose opinion she valued the most.

50 WAYS TO SHOW A CHARACTER
IS A GOOD PERSON

This is related to the list "100 Positive Character Traits." It shows some of the *best* traits on that list, like compassion, consideration, and tolerance, *in action*.

Sometimes, you want to let your readers know right away that a character is really a nice person, even if she or he has flaws. You might also have a moment in your story when a character realizes he misjudged a basically decent person. Here are a lot of ways to show a character has a good heart, rather than simply telling your reader that he does.

1. She says good morning to someone and asks how his weekend was.

2. He smiles at a stranger.

3. She listens to someone else's story—even if it's boring.

4. He sympathizes with someone's gripes—even petty ones.

5. She notices when someone's down and asks if everything's okay.

6. He treats an unpopular or weird person with respect.

7. She compliments someone's handiwork or a photo of his children.

8. He tells somebody that she's being too hard on herself.

9. She gives money to a panhandler when everyone else walks on by.

10. He knows the name of the elderly neighbor down the hallway from him, or the security guard at his company.

11. She gives directions to someone who is lost. Maybe she notices he looks confused and asks him if he needs help.

12. He calls his mom.

13. She visits her sick friend or her aging relative.

14. He takes care of a friend's baby or kid for the afternoon.

15. On her morning commute, she lets somebody merge in front of her.

16. When someone bumps into him, he says it's okay instead of getting annoyed.

17. When she has a legitimate customer complaint, she addresses it kindly rather than rudely.

18. He stands up for a sales associate or cashier being abused by a customer.

19. She donates blood.

20. He volunteers, formally or informally. He teaches a kid to read, or dishes out food at a community kitchen.

21. She holds the elevator door for someone—and tells him, "Take your time."

22. He gives his seat to somebody else on the bus.

23. She's nice to her dog or cat.

24. He helps catch someone else's dog or cat who got loose on the street.

25. She puts her shopping cart back where it's supposed to go.

26. He apologizes when he's made a mistake.

27. She shovels snow off her neighbor's sidewalk.

28. He leaves a great tip.

29. She writes a nice comment on someone's post or picture on social media.

30. He lets someone with just one or two items go ahead of him in line at the grocery store.

31. When someone in front of her in line at the grocery store is short a dollar, she chips in the difference.

32. He brings donuts to the office.

33. She buys lemonade from the neighbor kids' lemonade stand.

34. He declines to participate in gossip.

35. She gives credit to a co-worker.

36. He reacts to his whining child with patience and restraint.

37. When she shops for clothes, she picks up a dress that slips off the hanger and returns it to the rack.

38. When he accidentally breaks something in a store, he finds a sales associate so he can pay for it instead of walking away.

39. She defuses a conversation that's growing tense with a joke.

40. He goes to church.

41. She prays.

42. He helps someone jump start her car or helps when it's stuck in the snow.

43. When she and someone else start speaking at the same time, she says, "Go ahead."

44. He finds a recycling bin for his empty can or bottle.

45. She picks up a piece of trash on the sidewalk or in a hallway and throws it away.

46. He strikes up conversation with someone who's alone and looks lost at a social event.

47. She compliments a child on his art project or his outfit.

48. When he's running late in the morning, he turns back because he forgot to kiss his wife goodbye.

49. She calls her husband in the middle of the day, just to say "I love you."

50. He gives someone a hug.

25 WAYS TO SHOW A CHARACTER IS A JERK

This is related to the list "100 Negative Character Traits." It shows some of the *worst* traits on that list in action.

Once in a while, I'll read a book where the protagonist and all her friends keep talking about how awful a particular character is—but the character doesn't seem all that bad to me. If I'm supposed to like and root for the protagonist, then this is a real problem in a story. It makes me, as a reader, wonder if the protagonist judges people too harshly.

If a character is eventually going to do something terrible, most of the time, you don't want him doing it out of nowhere. Moreover, if you're writing a mystery or thriller, you may want to make one character seem suspicious, even if it turns out he's just an ordinary unpleasant person and not the bad guy.

Some of the things on this list are really mean, but some could also be done by a decent character on a bad day. Just don't let her off the hook for it.

1. She gives backhanded compliments.

    "That's a great picture of you. Your face looks slimmer."

2. He says something sexist or bigoted.

    It may be subtle—the kind of thing where no one corrects him, because they're asking themselves, "Did he mean what I think he meant?"

3. She shares a nasty rumor without being able to confirm it.

4. She's condescending to the server or the person doing her nails.

5. He sends back his order, even though it's fine.

    "This bagel is all the way toasted, but I said I wanted it *lightly* toasted."

6. He demeans his spouse, child, or friend in front of others.

   He might do it in the guise of a joke, but it's hurtful.

7. She takes up two spaces when she parks her car.

8. He parks in a spot reserved for the disabled, even though he is able-bodied.

   He might make the excuse that he's in a hurry, or he's only going to be a minute.

9. She honks other drivers, or even pedestrians, for minor infractions.

10. When he wins at something, he gloats.

11. She leaves a mess behind.

    She tosses her cigarette butt on the sidewalk or doesn't re-rack her weights at the gym.

12. He sexually harasses someone who is in no position to object.

    It may take the form of subtle innuendo or compliments that are over the line.

13. She doesn't say "thank you."

14. He says "no" instead of "no thanks."

15. She helps herself to someone else's food.

16. He borrows things without asking.

17. She insists on being addressed as "Doctor" or "Senator," if she is one.

18. He makes himself too comfortable.

    He sprawls out and takes up two seats on the subway, or he puts his feet up on someone else's coffee table.

19. She gives unsolicited and bossy advice.

20. He declines to sponsor a walkathon or order Girl Scout cookies.

21. He complains about crying babies or loud little kids.

22. She makes detailed and/or unreasonable demands.

    "I've attached a list of acceptable baby shower gifts. I don't want anything homemade or any stuffed animals."

23. He issues orders when most people would make requests.

24. She makes fun of people who aren't hurting anyone, either behind their backs or to their faces.

25. He never passes up the opportunity to show how smart or successful he is.

25 VERY COMMON JOBS

Are you trying to figure out how a character makes a living? Here are twenty-five very common jobs in the United States. Some of them are rarely depicted in novels and movies, and any of them can ground your story in reality. If your character has stress or money worries because of his or her job, many of your readers will be able to empathize.

If you are writing about a job that you've never done before, I recommend taking someone with that occupation out to lunch and interviewing them. A lot of people love to talk about their jobs. Not only will you learn interesting details, but you might even get a great idea for a scene or a subplot that you would have never come up with on your own. YouTube also has many videos of people talking about their day-to-day jobs, so it can be another great resource.

1. Retail sales associates.

   Anyone who deals a lot with the public has some pretty interesting encounters.

2. Cashiers.

3. Cooks.

   They work not only in restaurants, but also in the cafeterias of schools, hospitals, and some companies.

4. Nurses.

   This job can naturally provide some drama in your story. Your character could be a registered nurse, a licensed practical nurse, or licensed vocational nurse.

5. Servers.

   A lot of readers either work as waiters and waitresses or have done so in the past, so they'll be able to relate.

6. Warehouse workers.

   They may prepare orders, pack boxes, and move freight. They might also take deliveries by truck to their destinations.

7. Secretaries and administrative assistants.

8. Janitors and cleaners.

   The majority of people in these jobs work evening shifts, and because the job is usually outsourced, some may work in more than one building every night. Janitors and cleaners may work in schools, office buildings, banks, hospitals, and even outdoor places such as amusement parks.

9. Office clerks.

   They might be answering phones, entering data, maintaining spreadsheets, making copies, or keeping records.

10. Grade school and high school teachers.

11. Truck drivers.

    This includes people who drive heavy freight across the country, and people who deliver furniture and other goods across town.

12. Nurse's aides and attendants.

    People in these jobs may work at assisted living facilities or nursing homes, hospitals, or hospices.

13. Sales representatives.

    A sales rep may spend a lot of time on the phone. Depending on her company, she may need to travel a lot to meet with clients.

14. Teacher assistants.

15. Retail store managers.

16. Mechanics.

    A mechanic may work on cars at an auto dealership or a repair shop. Some specialize in diesel engines and work on buses or trucks.

17. Nursery school teachers and day care providers.

18. Accountants and auditors.

19. Maids and housekeepers.

Unlike janitors, people in these jobs work in private homes.

20. Landscaping and groundskeeping workers.

21. Construction workers.

22. Computer support specialists.

They are otherwise known as information technology specialists, or I/T.

23. Bank tellers.

24. Security guards.

25. Software developers.

A developer is likely to work on a team. He might work on something new, or he might adapt or improve an existing program.

25 POTENTIALLY HIGH-PAYING JOBS

It sometimes annoys me when characters in movies, TV shows, and novels have gotten rich doing something that almost no one gets rich doing. While almost anything is possible, this does take me out of the story, at least for a few moments.

The most common reason to be rich is to be born into a rich family. However, here are some jobs for self-made characters. Not everyone with these occupations is wealthy, but it's certainly a possibility.

Doctors make a lot of money in general, but I've highlighted some particularly well-paying fields. This list ranges from the outrageously rich to the simply prosperous, and it's not in order.

1. Tech entrepreneur.

   Many tech entrepreneurs fail or enjoy only modest success, but this is still a great choice for a young billionaire.

2. Star professional athlete.

3. A-list actor.

   This one is a little obvious, and so is the next one:

4. CEO of a huge corporation.

   Keep in mind that a CEO of a giant company is most likely to be in his or her fifties or older, unless he started the company himself (see #1.)

5. CFO of a huge corporation.

   The person in charge of managing the financial side of the company is generally doing well financially herself. Again, it usually takes a person many years to reach this level.

6. Real estate investor.

Many rich people got that way through buying and selling property.

7. Investment banker.

At the managing director or senior VP level, especially, investment bankers can make a lot of money.

8. Orthopedic surgeon.

9. Cardiac surgeon.

10. Petroleum engineer.

This job involves making sure that the drilling process is done correctly. Petroleum geologists, who help oil companies figure out where to drill in the first place, can also make a great salary.

11. Gastroenterologist.

12. Psychiatrist.

Both psychologists and psychiatrists do pretty well. Psychiatrists are the ones with medical degrees who can prescribe medications.

13. M&A attorney.

Lawyer salaries vary wildly, and many aren't rich. Attorneys who work in corporate mergers and acquisitions can make a lot more than most, especially if they are partners at big firms. Note that it usually takes at least ten years to make partner.

14. Plastic Surgeon.

This is an extremely profitable field.

15. CEO of a large nonprofit.

This might not be one that immediately comes to mind, but some CEOs of big nonprofit organizations make huge salaries.

---

16. IP attorney.

    Intellectual property litigators are often handsomely compensated, particularly if they are partners in big firms.

17. Anesthesiologist.

    They make sure you're not awake for surgery, and make sure you can still wake up afterward—two very important things.

18. Dentist.

19. Orthodontist.

20. Neurosurgeon.

21. Marketing or management consultant.

    The person the company flies in to tell them everything they are doing wrong is often doing quite well for herself.

22. Senior marketing manager.

    At large companies, this can be a very lucrative job.

23. I/T manager.

    Ditto.

24. Obstetrician/gynecologist.

25. Creative director in fashion or retail.

25 JOBS THAT SOUND LIKE FUN

For this list, I asked a lot of people what jobs had always sounded appealing to them. I told them to set practical considerations aside.

I'm guessing that, like most jobs, these have their joys and their challenges. However, they are the kinds of occupations that a lot of people hear about and think, "That must be so much fun!"

Giving your protagonist one of these jobs may attract some readers right away. If it's something that sounds like fun to you, experiencing it in your imagination might make your whole story more enjoyable to write. These aren't in any particular order!

1. Sports announcer.

2. Owner of a bakery.

   Some people imagine specializing in pies, cupcakes, cookies, or cakes, which they might decorate.

3. Singer.

   I believe "rock star" falls under this category.

4. Voiceover actor.

5. Owner of a bed and breakfast.

   It's amazing how many people have a fantasy of doing this one.

6. Airline or helicopter pilot.

7. Wedding planner.

   This is probably a difficult job, but somehow it's inherently adorable.

8. Librarian.

9. Owner of a bookstore or comic book shop.

10. Travel writer.

   I also heard "TV host on a travel show." The idea of globetrotting for a living naturally appeals to people.

11. Photographer.

   Specifically, "travel photographer" and "nature photographer."

12. Interior designer.

13. Fashion designer.

14. Character actor at a big amusement park.

   When I started thinking about this list, this was the first thing that came into my head. I wasn't the only one.

15. Archaeologist.

16. Beach lifeguard.

   This makes sense—lots of people love the beach. In addition, if you're a lifeguard, you're likely to be in good shape. I also heard "scuba dive instructor," and I bet "surfing instructor" would rank right up there, too.

17. Backup dancer.

18. Dog day care owner.

   For those of us who adore all kinds of pups, this sounds lovely. Veterinarian came up as well.

19. Floral designer or flower shop owner.

20. Zoologist or marine biologist.

21. Brewmaster.

22. Developer of computer or video games.

23. Journalist.

24. FBI profiler.

This may be intense, but people still think it sounds like fun.

25. Personal shopper.

50 COMMON HOBBIES AND INTERESTS

Our passions are a crucial part of who we are. What do the people in your story love to do? How do they like to spend their time off? The hobbies and interests listed here are popular, and one of them might be perfect for your character.

1. Watching TV.

   Obviously, most people do this. *Not* watching TV is rare enough to be a distinctive trait of a character. However, if the person in your story is a huge fan of a particular show or genre of shows, that can be a big part of who she is. She might even follow the lives of the actors or go to conventions.

2. Travel.

   Your character may have a passion and the means to explore exotic lands, or he may find adventure on thrifty road trips.

3. Cooking.

   While many people prepare simple and basic meals, some take it to a whole different level and collect recipes like mad, even when they're not in the kitchen.

4. Baking.

   Sometimes this goes along with cooking, but someone in your story may be focused mostly on making muffins, cakes, cookies, and pies.

5. Playing sports.

   Your character doesn't have to possess incredible skills (though she might) to be really into her softball or roller derby team.

6. Watching sports.

   Lots of people enjoy watching sports on television, in real life, or both. You may have someone in your story who is a superfan of a particular team and never misses a game for years on end.

7. Playing videogames.

   All kinds of people spend hours at this every week, and some of them make friends or find spouses this way.

8. Playing board games.

   "Game night" with friends or family may be a weekly fixture in your character's life.

9. Photography.

   Thanks to digital cameras, camera phones, and easy sharing, more people enjoy this hobby than ever. Some people take a photo every day to document their lives, share lots of self-portraits, or seek out impressive photo opportunities.

10. Shopping.

    Everyone has to do it to some extent, unless he has somebody to do it for him. However, you might have a character who delights in finding rare items, great bargains, or unique and stylish accessories.

11. Connecting on social networks.

    Most people do it a little, but some people have many social media accounts and chat almost nonstop.

12. Sewing.

    Making clothes, quilts, or smaller projects is a very popular hobby.

13. Knitting or crocheting.

    Your character might always be working on a scarf and might have a formidable stash of pretty yarn.

14. Gardening.

   He might grow flowers, food, or both. If he's a city dweller, he might be part of a community garden.

15. Home décor or home improvement.

   She may spend a lot of her time getting design ideas or buying tools, tiles, and paint.

16. Reading.

   Although it's a solitary activity, many people join book clubs to read and discuss.

17. Watching movies.

   For some, it's a once-in-a-while thing, but for your character, it might be an obsession. He might have a particular genre he loves, and he might be able to tell people all about production and trivia.

18. Fishing.

19. Hunting.

   People who hunt often enjoy fishing as well.

20. Running.

21. Hiking.

22. Going to church.

   Besides attending regular services, people attend Bible studies and fellowship groups, teach Sunday school classes, and sing in church choirs.

23. Volunteering.

   This also might be through a church, or she might log hours at the local food bank or animal shelter.

24. Going to the gym.

He might be really into lifting weights or going to spin classes.

25. Doing yoga.

Your character might do this on her own, or she might go to a yoga studio.

26. Golf.

27. Woodworking.

This is more popular with men, but there is no reason your female character couldn't be into it.

28. Making jewelry.

Although more women do this craft, plenty of guys are into it too.

29. Riding a motorcycle.

This might be a solitary pastime, or your character might be in a motorcycle club.

30. Riding a bicycle.

Again, this might be done alone or as a social activity—with a spouse, the whole family, or with friends.

31. Home beer brewing.

32. Camping.

A character who loves the great outdoors is likely to find some adventures.

33. Playing a musical instrument.

She might perform somewhere regularly. She also might be in some kind of band or orchestra.

34. Clubbing.

She might love meeting attractive new people, or she might just love to dance.

35. Playing poker.

He might do this regularly with friends, and/or he might enter competitive tournaments.

36. Boating.

37. Horseback riding.

If she has a horse, it may be a big part of her identity.

38. Theatre.

Your character might be involved in local productions as an actor or in a behind-the-scenes role.

39. Tennis.

40. Skiing.

41. Writing.

Many people write poetry or stories, or keep up regular blogs.

42. Restoring classic cars.

43. Genealogy.

If he's really into researching his family tree, it may lead him to visiting county archives or distant cemeteries and discovering surprising things about his ancestors.

44. Political activism.

She may support a candidate, a party, or a cause. She might attend rallies or meetings, or organize letter-writing campaigns.

45. Collecting.

There is almost no end of things that people love to collect, but they include coins, stamps, Christmas ornaments, baseball cards, comic books, toys, and certain types of figurines, including action figures.

46. Geocaching.

People hide things, and other people use GPS to find them.

47. Drawing and painting.

48. Coaching.

She might coach her daughter's softball team, or a kids' soccer team through her local YMCA.

49. Swimming.

50. Entertaining.

Hosting dinner parties, cocktail hours, and big bashes may your character's mission in life. Sounds like fun!

100 CHARACTER QUIRKS

Have you ever noticed that when you miss somebody, you miss some of the weirdest little things about her? A person's quirks can really stick in your mind. The same is true with fictional characters. Here is a big collection of habits, rituals, attitudes, and favorite things that will likely remind you of some people you know—and no doubt make you think of other quirks as well.

1. She smiles all the time, even when talking about something awful.

2. He cracks his knuckles frequently.

3. She only eats one thing on her plate at a time. Instead of alternating between the steak and the baked potato, for instance, she finishes off one and then attacks the other.

4. He always knows what the weather is going to be like, not only in his own locale, but in other parts of the continent as well. He just really likes weather.

5. She has her headphones on almost constantly, maybe because she's shy or antisocial.

6. When she sits at a table or desk and she's bored, she spins quarters on their sides. She might do it with her wedding ring.

7. He texts his mom or his boyfriend to say "I love you" before he flies anywhere, because he's scared he'll die in a plane crash.

8. He clears out his search history every time he's done using the computer, although he never looks at anything scandalous.

9. She can't step out of the house, even to take out the trash, unless she is wearing makeup.

10. He shares quotes from movies, pop songs, or famous thinkers of the past. Or all three.

11. She saves lots of boxes and bubble wrap in case she ever has to mail a gift or suddenly move to a new apartment.

12. He hits the snooze button on his alarm clock at least twice every morning.

13. She has trypophobia. Objects with small holes, close together, freak her out.

14. He puts hot sauce on almost everything.

15. She eats one particular snack food, or drinks one particular beverage, to excess.

16. The sight of a hypodermic needle makes him woozy.

17. She occasionally adopts an accent other than her own—British, Southern—for comic effect.

18. He cannot walk past a dog without talking to it and petting it.

19. She sleeps with a teddy bear.

20. When he's driving, he often doesn't notice when the light has turned green because he's a daydreamer.

21. She cannot parallel park to save her life.

22. His sneezes are so loud that they terrify people.

23. She frequently talks in her sleep.

24. He plans all of his outfits for the week on Sunday night.

25. She has nine shirts that are basically the same shirt.

26. He loves routine. He does the same things at the same time every day.

27. She believes in ghosts, past lives, or other supernatural phenomena.

28. He believes in obscure herbal remedies for health issues.

29. She always smacks her gum.

30. He is uncomfortable with silence, so he keeps up a steady stream of chatter even if he has nothing to say.

31. She is never on time for anything.

32. He is so early for everything it sometimes leads to awkwardness.

33. She has trouble recognizing faces, unless she knows people very well.

34. He has no sense of direction whatsoever.

35. She says "rabbit rabbit" first thing in the morning, on the first day of the month, for good luck.

36. He wears a particular hat or jersey when his team is playing to help them win.

37. She listens to an unusual genre of music for pleasure, such as marching band recordings, or Christmas music all year.

38. When he's driving, he sings along dramatically with his music and dances in his seat.

39. She carries a planner or a journal and jots in it frequently.

40. He smokes a cigar every Friday evening when he comes home from work.

41. Her desk is covered with empty paper coffee cups or empty cans of soda.

42. She doesn't talk about herself. If someone asks about her, she gives a short answer and quickly changes the subject.

43. He changes the topic of conversation frequently because he has a short attention span.

44. She worries a lot about germs.

45. He compliments people profusely.

46. She's always cold. She wraps up in blankets and begs people to turn off the air conditioning.

47. He's a vegan.

48. She has trouble making eye contact.

49. He borrows things and never returns them.

50. She changes her hairstyle and hair color often.

51. Children, dogs, food, and beverages are not allowed in his car.

52. Because she's so sentimental, she gets choked up easily.

53. He is a walking encyclopedia of mostly useless trivia.

54. She takes off her bra while she watches TV at home...and sometimes leaves the bra on the couch.

55. He goes barefoot whenever possible.

56. True crime stories fascinate her.

57. He's easily upset by noise.

58. She gets up every morning before the crack of dawn.

59. He's a night owl, and possibly an insomniac.

60. She's convinced that society is going to hell in a handbasket.

61. He talks to plants or possibly inanimate objects as though they were sentient beings.

62. She hates talking on the phone and avoids it whenever possible.

63. He wears a little too much cologne.

64. She apologizes when she has done nothing wrong.

65. He believes he's always being slighted, overlooked, or ill-used.

66. No matter what the circumstances, she likes her chances for success.

67. He always drinks right out of the milk carton.

68. She will write something that she has already done on her to-do list so she can check it off.

69. He doodles in meetings or during class.

70. She talks so quietly, it's hard to hear what she's saying.

71. He puts so much cream and sugar in his coffee that it's barely coffee.

72. She's obsessed with politics, including the petty shenanigans.

73. He always has to be out doing something and gets cranky if he stays at home a couple of nights in a row.

74. When she texts, she uses lots of emoticons. Even her emails have a lot of smiley faces.

75. He judges people who dress provocatively.

76. She judges people who drive expensive cars or live in fancy houses.

77. He does pushups and sit-ups every morning.

78. She has an elaborate dental hygiene routine.

79. He meditates.

80. She jiggles her leg constantly whenever she's sitting down.

81. He takes lots of pictures of people.

82. She puts bumper stickers all over her car.

83. He makes decisions by drawing up comprehensive lists of pros and cons.

84. She makes decisions by flipping a coin.

85. He imagines fantastic scenarios in his head—heroic, horrible, or hilarious.

86. She flirts with pretty much everyone.

87. He tells very long stories.

88. She loves to make spreadsheets, graphs, and charts.

89. He makes everything into a competition and takes casual games way too seriously.

90. She is horrible with money and frequently has her services cut off because she forgot to pay the bills.

91. He gives odd and sometimes incomprehensible gifts.

92. She always has some new business venture or get-rich-quick scheme.

93. Large crowds make him nervous.

94. She loves finding bargains, and tells people about them.

95. He constantly interacts on social media.

96. She's always making food for people and trying to get them to eat.

97. He frequently misplaces his glasses.

98. She is brilliant at multi-tasking. For instance, she can carry on a phone conversation while emailing someone else.

99. He's nostalgic for his high school or college years.

100. She cyberstalks her exes to see how they're doing.

ONE MORE VERY IMPORTANT LIST:

10 REASONS WHY YOU SHOULD WRITE THAT STORY

1. Because nobody else can write it but you.

    Your beliefs, your knowledge, your brain chemistry, plus the sum total of all your experiences, make you absolutely unique in the world. (Some would argue your very soul is unique, but souls are a matter of opinion.) They mean that nobody can write the *exact* story you can. If you don't write it, it will never exist.

2. Because you're not alone.

    If you're into it, someone else out there will be, too. Even if you believe your story is niche or unusual, other people share some of your interests or experiences. The audience may be small, or it may be huge. Either way, it exists. If your story is different, the people who love that kind of story will be all the more grateful to find it.

3. Because your life will go by either way.

    Some people worry about how much time it will take them to finish a project. What if it takes a whole year? What if it takes three? Three years from now, you will be three years older, and you can do that with or without a finished story (or two, or ten.) Your choice.

4. Because you're not too young.

    If you're young, it's the perfect time to learn. You don't need to wait until college or grad school. You may not need to go to college or grad school. If you work hard and seek out opportunities to learn, you can start becoming proficient at your craft right now.

5. Because you're not too old.

    Writing isn't like Olympic figure skating or being in a boy band. As long as your mind is still working, you can write a story. Harriet Doerr published her debut novel, *Stones for Ibarra*, at the age of 74. It won a National Book Award. As you get older, you know more about life and have had more experiences, and that will only make your writing better.

6. Because you have the right.

    Some people tell themselves that they aren't smart enough or creative enough to attempt writing—even when they really want to. They wonder if they can tell extraordinary stories when their lives are so ordinary. Others worry that people will judge them for writing ("Who do you think you are?"), or judge them for writing in a certain genre ("Comic books, really?") You have as much right as anybody else to tell stories, plus the right to ignore anyone who says otherwise.

7. Because it doesn't have to be perfect.

    Perfectionism can keep people from daring to write their story— or to finish it. If it's your very first story, it doesn't ever have to be good. Nobody gets into the NBA after playing one basketball game. Nobody paints a museum-worthy masterpiece the first time they pick up a brush. Learning and struggling aren't shameful, but reasons to feel proud.

    Some of the greatest stories have flaws that everyone acknowledges. Good writing isn't just about getting rid of flaws, but also about building on your strengths—and entertaining, enlightening, and inspiring.

Besides, no matter how proficient you get, no story ever has to be good in the rough draft stage. It's the final draft that counts.

8. Because you'll never know how good it can be until you try.

   It might be brilliant.

9. Because you have complete control over it.

   If you're like most people, you don't get to control everything in your life. The behavior of the people around you, the stock market, the weather—for better or worse, you have to just deal with these things.

   In your story, you are in charge. Like an all-powerful deity, you can create an entire world, and the people who populate it. With very few exceptions, nobody can take your story away from you.

10. Because if you don't, then later you might wish you had.

   You don't ever want to look back with regrets. So write your story, and have fun!

Thanks for reading *Master Lists for Writers*. If you enjoyed this book, please leave a review!

Follow emy blog, bryndonovan.com, for future lists for writers and other inspirational and practical posts about creativity. I would love to connect.